MYTHS AND LEGEND

ODIN
THE VIKING ALLFATHER

STEVEN S. LONG
ILLUSTRATED BY ᵃRU-MOR

First published in Great Britain in 2015 by Osprey Publishing,
Kemp House, Chawley Park, Cumnor Hill, Oxford, OX2 9PH, UK
4301 21st. St., Suite 220, Long Island City, NY 11101, USA
E-mail: info@ospreypublishing.com

Osprey Publishing is part of the Osprey Group

The Publisher has made every attempt to secure appropriate permissions for material reproduced in this book. If there has been any oversight we will be happy to recify the situation and written submission should be made to the publishers.

A CIP catalog record for this book is available from the British Library

Print ISBN: 978 4728 0806 6
PDF e-book ISBN: 978 1 4728 0807 3
EPUB e-book ISBN: 978 1 4728 0808 0

Typeset in Garamond Pro and Myriad Pro

Originated by PDQ Media, Bungay, UK
Printed in China through Worldprint Ltd.

15 16 17 18 19   10 9 8 7 6 5 4 3 2 1

Osprey Publishing is supporting the Woodland Trust, the UK's leading woodland conservation charity, by funding the dedication of trees.

www.ospreypublishing.com

CONTENTS

INTRODUCTION

Odin, often referred to by his epithet "All-Father," is the ruler and military leader of the *Aesir*, the pantheon of the ancient Norsemen. A god of war, wisdom, and wizardry, he can see everything happening in the Nine Worlds from his throne, the Hlidskjalf. In his hall, Valhalla, he hosts the *einherjar*, the fallen warriors and heroes of mankind who will fight with the gods in Ragnarok, the final battle against the giants.

Although he is not as well-known as his mighty son Thor, the god of thunder, Odin appears frequently in Norse myths. While Thor enjoyed wide popularity as a god of the common man, kings, warriors, and poets revered Odin, thus ensuring him a prominent place in legend.

A statue of Odin in all his glory. (Ivy Close Images / Alamy)

Although Odin hasn't experienced as much ongoing interest as Thor in the modern world, he nevertheless remains a powerful, archetypical figure – the wise, one-eyed king with ravens on his shoulders and wolves at his feet, ready to render judgment or go to war, fiercely protective of his people. In his guise as a robed wanderer with a wide-brimmed hat and a staff he has influenced, among other things, J.R.R. Tolkien's character Gandalf.

This book examines Odin in all his aspects, from the earliest tales of Norse myth and legend to his modern day appearances in novels, comic books, and games.

The Norse Gods

While Odin stands first and foremost among the Aesir (literally "The Gods"), he's by no means the only Norse deity. Some who appear prominently in the main sources include:

Baldur (also spelled Balder or Baldr): the god of peace, truth, and light. He's one of Odin's sons by Frigg. Everyone throughout the Nine Worlds loves Baldur. Loki's vicious murder of him casts a pall over the Aesir and is the first step on the road to Ragnarok.

Frey: a god of sunlight and fertility. He, his sister Freya, and their father Njord are members of the *Vanir*, a race of deities who live in Vanaheim. These three came to live with the Aesir to seal the peace after the Aesir–Vanir war. Frey rides the shining golden boar Gullinbursti, and owns the ship *Skidbladnir* which is big enough to carry all of the Aesir but can fold down until it's small enough to fit in Frey's pocket. He lives in Alfheim, where he rules the elves.

Freya (or Freyja): goddess of beauty and love. She wears the fabulous necklace Brisingamen which makes her even more beautiful, and also owns a cloak of falcon feathers that the other gods occasionally borrow if they need to fly somewhere. When she mourns for her lost husband Odur, she cries tears of pure gold.

Frigg (or Frigga): Odin's wife. She spins the clouds on her spinning wheel.

Heimdall: the sentinel of the gods. He stands watch at the head of Bifrost, the Rainbow Bridge. He can see things 100 miles away as clearly as if he were next to them and can hear the grass growing down on Midgard. When he senses danger approaching, he blows the Gjallarhorn to alert the Aesir.

The Norns who decide the fates of both humans and gods. (Ivy Close Images / Alamy)

Loki: a mischievous trickster god who becomes more and more malicious as the cycle of Norse myth progresses. Eventually he turns against the Aesir, murders Baldur, and suffers painful imprisonment until Ragnarok, when he breaks free and joins the giants to fight the gods. The goddess Hel, the fearsome Midgard Serpent, and the monstrous wolf Fenris are Loki's children.

Loki was not originally a god. He is the son of the giant Farbauti and the giantess or goddess Laufey. His handsome looks and cleverness attracted Odin's attention, and they became blood brothers, with Odin inviting him to live with him in Asgard. In some respects you can think of Loki as the "dark side" of Odin – the All-Father's wisdom and magic turned to cunning, treachery, and selfishness.

Thor: the hot-tempered god of thunder and the Aesir's mightiest warrior. The son of Odin and the earth goddess Jord, he wields the red-hot thunderbolt hammer Mjolnir which returns to his hand after he throws it and can slay a *jotun* (giant) with a single blow. Many myths describe his battles against Asgard's enemies.

Tyr: the god of war and victory. He appears most prominently in the myth of the chaining of Fenris, when he sacrifices his right hand to ensure that the gigantic wolf remains captive until Ragnarok.

The Nine Worlds

The cosmology of Norse myth describes the Nine Worlds, nine realms inhabited by various beings. The eddas don't describe this setting consistently, so there is some debate regarding whether certain names refer to places that are separate worlds or part of an existing world, or are simply alternate terms for an existing world.

Uppermost among the Nine Worlds are the three realms of Asgard, Vanaheim, and Alfheim.

Asgard is the glittering, wondrous home of the Aesir. There they have their halls and amuse themselves with games, sports, feasting, and dalliance. Bifrost, the Rainbow Bridge, connects it with Midgard. A strong wall surrounds it.

Vanaheim is the home of the Vanir, fertility gods who receive little attention in Norse myth other than mentions of their war with the Aesir and the subsequent exchange of hostages that brought Frey, Freya, and Njord to Asgard.

Alfheim, the beautiful world of the *Ljosalfar*, or "Light Elves". Frey lives there and rules them.

In the "middle" of the Nine Worlds are the three "terrestrial" realms of Midgard, Svartalfheim, and Jotunheim.

Midgard ("Middle-earth") is the world where humanity lives; its creation is described below.

Svartalfheim, which lies below Midgard, is the realm of the *Dvergar*, or dwarves (also known as the *Svartalfar*, "Dark Elves"). The gods journey there when they need the dwarves to make something for them.

Jotunheim, the land of the jotuns (giants), trolls, and other monsters. Gods and heroes, particularly Thor, often travel there in search of adventure or to battle jotuns. The jotuns in turn enjoy pelting Midgard with boulders and ice whenever they can.

Yggdrasil, the World Tree. (Mary Evans Picture Library / Alamy)

The "lowest" level of the Nine Worlds contains the most unpleasant places in Norse myth: Hel; Niflheim; and Muspelheim.

Hel, the land of the dead, is the domain of the goddess of the same name. Anyone who dies of old age, illness, an accident, or the like goes there; chosen warriors and heroes end up in Valhalla.

Niflheim ("The Dark World") is a land of ice, cold, and darkness. Nothing kind or helpful lives there; indeed, very little lives there at all.

Muspelheim is a world of fire and heat. Fire giants dwell there; the cruel and mighty Surtur is their king.

Connecting all of the Nine Worlds is Yggdrasil, the World Ash Tree. It has three main roots. The first emerges next to Asgard, at Urd's Well where the three *Norns,* or Fates, weave the threads of the lives of men. The second plunges deep into Niflheim to emerge at the spring Hvergelmir. The fierce dragon Nidhogg gnaws at this root in an unending effort to destroy the World Ash. The third root grows into Jotunheim and comes out at Mimir's Well, whose waters grant wisdom.

Sources Of Norse Myth

Many medieval manuscripts and folk tales refer to the Norse myths in some way, but the principal sources for Norse mythology are the *Poetic Edda* and the *Prose Edda*.

The Poetic Edda

The *Poetic Edda*, also known as the *Elder Edda*, is a collection of Old Norse poems and lays from various sources. It derives primarily from the *Codex Regius*, or *Konungsbok* ("The King's Book"), a manuscript thought to have been written in the 1200s even though there is no proof of its location or ownership until 1643.

Rather than forming one unified narrative, the various poems in the *Poetic Edda* touch on a wide variety of Norse myths and heroic legends. In some places the verses recount a myth in detail, but in other places they only mention a tale briefly. Of its approximately three dozen sections, six have a close connection to Odin:

The *Voluspa*, or "Prophecy of the Volva," in which Odin uses his magic to summon a *volva*, or seeress, from the dead to appear before the gods and reveal certain wisdom to them.

The *Havamal*, or "Sayings of Har," a collection of wisdom, advice, and proverbs conveyed by Odin to men. It also includes a section where Odin lists some of the magic spells he knows.

The *Vafthrudnismal*, or "Lay of Vafthrudnir," in which Odin challenges the eponymous giant to a contest of lore.

The *Grimnismal*, or "Lay of Grimnir," the story of how Odin punishes an unworthy king.

One-eyed Odin with his ravens, Hugin ("thought") and Munin ("memory"), from an 18th-century Icelandic manuscript. (PD)

The *Harbarzljod*, or "Lay of Harbard," in which a disguised Odin refuses to ferry Thor across an inlet and engages him in a bragging contest.

Baldrs draumr, or "Baldur's Dream," when Odin rides to the gates of Hel to raise a volva from her grave to prophesy about the strange dreams his son Baldur has recently had.

Lastly, Odin appears in the *Reginsmal* ("Lay of Regin") and some of the other "heroic legends" sections of the *Poetic Edda* when he interacts with the Volsungs and other Viking heroes.

The Prose Edda

The *Prose Edda*, sometimes called the *Younger Edda* or *Snorra Edda*, was written by Snorri Sturluson (1179–1241), an Icelandic politician, historian, and scholar, around the year 1220. Drawing heavily on earlier sources (including the *Poetic Edda*), it consists of a prologue and three parts.

In the prologue Snorri, a Christian, attempts to explain Norse mythology through euhemerization (treating myths as historical accounts exaggerated and distorted over time). He connects it to Greek myth by describing the Norse gods as heroes who fled the sack of Troy and traveled to northern Europe. There they became kings, and through time and tales transformed into gods.

The first section, *Gylfaginning* ("The Deluding of Gylfi"), presents extensive mythological information through an unusual story framework. After being tricked by a Norse goddess, King Gylfi of Sweden journeys to Asgard to find out if the gods accomplish everything through deception and magic. Unfortunately the gods trick him along the way and he winds up at a mysterious palace. There he meets three men seated on thrones who call themselves Har, Jafnhar, and Thridji (High, Just As High, and Third) – all manifestations of Odin. As Gylfi questions them he learns about the world, particularly how the gods created it and how it will suffer destruction at Ragnarok.

The second section, the *Skaldskaparmal* ("The Language of Poetry"), concerns the style and nature of Norse poetry. The sea giant Aegir speaks with Bragi, the god of poetry, on the subject. In particular the dialogue focuses on *kennings*, poetic metaphors common to Norse literature. For example, the "whale-road" is the ocean," the "slayer of giants" is Thor, and the "hanged god" is Odin. As he explains what the kennings mean Bragi tells many myths.

The third section, the *Hattatal* ("List of Verse Forms"), isn't included in many modern translations. It demonstrates and systematizes the forms of Norse poetry, but features no significant mythological information.

Modern scholars have studied how Snorri's Christianity affected the value of his work, but have reached no definitive conclusions. For some, his Christian perspective makes it difficult or impossible to derive meaningful, accurate information about Old Norse religion, customs, and myths from the *Prose Edda*. Others argue that the "Christianization" of Norse myth and practice began long before Snorri's time, so determining which aspects of Christianization are his fault and which he was essentially the victim of isn't really possible. Regardless, most scholars give him credit for his work as a recorder and mythographer. Fortunately for lovers of mythology, the issue is largely moot; Snorri's myths remain highly entertaining.

Snorri also wrote the *Heimskringla*, a history of the kings of Norway. One section, the *Ynglinga Saga*, chronicles the earliest periods of history and features some mythological information. Odin makes occasional appearances in other stories in the book as well.

ODIN'S ATTRIBUTES

Given the importance of his role in Norse mythology, Odin has inspired depictions in paintings and sculpture for hundreds of years. Both historically and in modern sources, artists usually portray Odin as a tall, regal-looking man with a full head of shoulder-length hair and a thick beard. His hair and beard are most often colored grey, but brown, brownish-blond, and reddish-brown aren't unknown.

When shown as a king, ruler of the Aesir, or god of war, Odin typically wears burnished chainmail, a golden eagle-winged helmet, and a blue cloak. A heavy gold arm-ring, Draupnir, adorns his upper right arm, and he holds his spear Gungnir. When he's seated on his throne his ravens Hugin and Munin perch on his shoulders and his wolves Freki and Geri sit at his feet.

After Odin visits Mimir and sacrifices his left eye for a drink from the jotun's well, he usually covers the empty socket with strands of his hair, but some depictions simply show it as a dark orbit. Modern illustrators often cover it with some sort of eyepatch or part of a helmet – such as Sir Anthony Hopkins wears when portraying Odin in the movies *Thor* and *Thor: The Dark World.*

In some Norse myths Odin travels to Midgard, Jotunheim, or other worlds in search of information or wisdom. As a "simple wanderer," Odin looks like an elderly man wearing ordinary clothing and a dark blue cloak. His hair and beard are grey, with strands over the missing left eye. He covers his head either with the hood of his cloak or with a tall, wide-brimmed hat. In the place of his spear Gungnir he carries a traveler's staff.

Role and Purpose

Odin is a multifaceted god who has several roles in Norse mythology and religion. As one scholar aptly put it, he is "complex and many-sided to an extreme degree." First and foremost he's the leader of the Aesir in both peace and war – their king or chief. This position comes to him not only because he is the eldest of the Norse gods (and the father of many of them), but because of his wisdom and power. Unlike Zeus in Greek mythology the Norse tales never explicitly describe Odin as more powerful than the other Aesir (either individually or collectively), but the implication exists. Between his magic, weapons, wisdom, insight, and awe-inspiring presence, few if any of the other gods would dare risk his wrath, much less stand against him.

Odin also serves the Aesir (and humanity) by acquiring valuable resources from the giants – the forces of chaos and nature unrestrained – so the gods can put them to better use. Through wit, deception, or power he takes what he needs from the giants, such as the magic mead of poetry, to enrich and empower the gods while weakening their foes. In the words of Margaret Clunies Ross, Odin is the "deity *par excellence* who embodies the questing spirit of the gods and the ruthless intelligence that allows them to exploit the natural resources of worlds beyond their direct control."

God of War

Odin is a god of war and warriors, particularly of the kings and lords who lead men into battle. The Vikings were often a warlike and aggressive people, so it comes as no surprise that the greatest of their deities was a war god. The *skalds* described how Odin, accompanied by his Valkyries, rode his horse Sleipnir to a battlefield where two armies contended. After looking over both sides, he chose which side should win, then threw his spear Gungnir over the heads of the warriors destined to lose. Odin used his wisdom and foresight to select the most deserving fighters to win a battle, but the decision wasn't always easy. Sometimes he favored weaker warriors so the stronger ones would die and come join him in Valhalla, or granted victory to a hero he favored despite the odds against that warrior.

Mortals could sometimes trick him, too. For example, Paul the Deacon's *Historia Langobardorum* recounts how two great peoples clashed. Odin thought them both worthy to win and couldn't make up his mind which

Odin riding with the Valkyries. (Ivy Close Images / Alamy)

should lose. At last he decided to favor whichever army took the field first the next morning. The women of one of the tribes prayed fervently to Frigg, who told them what to do. Following her advice the women arose early, put on armor, and took up weapons and shields. Finally each of them combed her hair to either side of her head and tied it under her chin so it looked like a beard. Then they assembled on the battlefield.

"Who are those long-beards?" Odin asked when he saw them.

"The army first on the field, to whom you said you'd give victory," Frigg replied. Odin threw Gungnir over the other army and the husbands of the disguised women won the battle – and earned the name Langobards, or Lombards ("Longbeards").

God of Wisdom and Magic

But Odin isn't just a god of warfare and slaughter. He also presides over wisdom, learning, and magic – a rare (if not unique) trait for the head of a pantheon in world mythology. In fact, some accounts (such as the *Ynglinga Saga*) emphasize his wisdom and skills over his military role. Many Norse myths focus on his efforts to gain wisdom or acquire new knowledge. He's especially interested in learning about the future so he can best guide the Aesir and avoid Ragnarok, the doom of the gods. But since abiding by one's own profound wisdom doesn't usually make for entertaining stories, in the Norse myths he often acts unwisely. Last but not least, Odin also dispenses wisdom to mortals, though unraveling the true meaning of what he says isn't always easy.

Odin possesses profound magical powers and lore. In addition to his knowledge of *galdrar* (magic incantations or "songs"), he discovered the enchanted runes, and at times consorted with witches, wizards, and necromancers. He also mastered *seidr*, a type of magic brought to the Aesir by Freya. The Norse regarded seidr, which they typically associated with women, as a compromising, humiliating, or "unmanly" practice. Working seidr magic didn't bother the All-Father, though. To him it was another tool with which he could help the gods and defeat their enemies. Loki mocks Odin about this in the *Poetic Edda*, stating:

> They say that with spells in Samsey once
> Like witches with charms didst thou work;
> And in witch's guise among men didst thou go;
> Unmanly thy soul must seem.

Shamanic God of the Dead

As a god of battle, Odin is associated with death. His powers to travel to Hel and to raise the dead from their graves reinforce this association, as does his connection to hanged men and the gallows. In that his valkyries take the spirits of dead warriors to Valhalla, he also functions as a sort of psychopomp.

And as commander of the einherjar (see below) he leads a host of the dead into battle.

Odin and his wife, Frigg. (Ivy Close Images / Alamy)

In this sense one can view Odin as having aspects of the shaman, and certainly his self-sacrifice on Yggdrasil (see next chapter) has a strong shamanic feel to it. So do his ability to inspire "ecstatic" states in some worshippers so they go berserk in battle, his frequent attempts to foresee or learn about the future, his power to ride his horse to the underworld, and his ability to change shape. Similarly, his leaving Asgard to wander the Nine Worlds to help the gods presents a mirror image of the typical shaman's role of traveling from the Mortal World to the Spirit World to help the mortal community. Sending Hugin and Munin, his ravens, out to observe the world each day may also reflect shamanic visions or travel.

On the other hand, archetypical shamanic tokens and powers such as dancing and healing have little or no connection to Odin, calling his standing as a shaman into doubt. (As one commentator puts it, "references to shamanistic practices... do not make [Odin] a shaman.") Some scholars argue that the suffering he endures to gain wisdom has more in common with the general ascetic practices found in many religions than with shamanism in particular.

God of Poetry and Eloquence

Odin is a god of poetry and eloquence. One reason he appears so often in

Frigg spins the clouds. (Ivy Close Images / Alamy)

the sagas is that he's the patron god of the poets who composed them. He can speak with grace or in finely-composed verse whenever he likes and can grant similar abilities to mortals; he's the source of the skalds' inspiration and creativity. He also obtained the magic mead of poetry for gods and men. Many kennings refer to this, describing verse as "the prize of Odin," "the gift of Grimnir," or "the holy cup of the raven-god."

The Duplicitous God

Because Odin's eternal purpose is to prepare for, and ultimately fight, Ragnarok, he sometimes does things that seem treacherous or deceptive. E.O.G. Turville-Petrie goes so far as to refer to him as a "god of lawlessness." He wants to acquire the best warriors for his army of einherjar, and if that means tricking or taking advantage of mortals, or inspiring them to states of reckless bravery or berserk fury so that they soon fall in battle, so be it.

Norse myth and saga often imply or state outright that many warriors distrust Odin, and for good reason. For example, in the *Havamal* Odin himself specifically points out that it's unwise to rely on him, saying bluntly, "How can his word be trusted?" Later in the *Poetic Edda*, Loki accuses him:

Be silent, Odin! not justly thou settest

Odin's Many Names

Scholars of Old Norse have proposed several different translations for Odin's name, such as "Spirit," "The Intoxicated One," "Frenzy," or "The Enraged One." All of these refer to his role as a source of inspiration (or possession) for poetry/eloquence/wisdom/magic, going berserk in battle, and similar ecstatic conditions.

But just one name isn't enough for such a powerful god with so many important aspects. Odin has more names and titles than any other Norse god – over 150 in the eddas and other skaldic sources. Some refer to his appearance, others to specific events from mythology or to his worship by mortals. Besides the well-known *Alfadir* ("All-Father"), some of them include:

Arhofdi ("Eagle Head")
Baleyg ("Flame-Eye")

Farmantyr ("God of Cargoes")
Fjolsvidr ("The Very Wise One")
Geirtyr ("Spear God")
Hangatyr ("The Hanging God")
Hrafnagud ("God of Ravens")
Runatyr ("God of Runes")
Sigfadir ("Father of Victory")
Ygg ("The Terrible One")

Additionally, Odin often uses false names when traveling in disguise. These include:

Vegtam ("Wanderer")
Gagnradr ("Giving Good Counsel")
Grímnir ("The Masked One").

> The fate of the fight among men;
> Oft gavst thou to him who deserved not the gift,
> To the baser, the battle's prize.

And Odin admits it:

> Though I gave to him who deserved not the gift,
> To the baser, the battle's prize.

He says much the same in the *Harbarzljod*, when he brags of fomenting wars and never making peace, and his conduct in *Hrolfs saga kraka* (see next chapter) also displays his Machiavellian nature. The hero Dag, who calls on Odin for help and receives it, nevertheless says, "Odin alone caused all the misfortune for he cast hostile runes between the kinsmen."

Sonatorrek, the famed skald Egil Skallagrimsson's lament about the death of his two sons, movingly addresses this darker side of Odin. It describes Egil's personal relationship with, and thoughts about, Odin in a way that's unique in Old Norse literature. Portraying the All-Father as a grim shadow looming over the lives of mortals, he says that he doesn't worship Odin willingly, though he admits Odin has granted him wonderful gifts – his abilities as a skald, and the power to perceive enemies – in compensation. He considers the death of his son Gunnarr too harsh a price for Odin to take from a mortal who has served him loyally.

But while Odin's conduct may seem malicious or treacherous to mortals, he doesn't act without purpose. In the *Eiriksmal*, a fragmentary tenth-century skaldic poem, he provides an eloquent explanation for his conduct. When the hero Sigmund asks, "Why, then, didst rob [Eirik] of victory, since valiant thou thought'st him?" Odin responds, "Because a grey wolf glares at the dwellings of the gods." In other words, Odin needs the best warriors to fight Fenris, regardless of how unfair or cruel it may seem when he arranges their deaths so they can join him in Valhalla.

Odin's Family

Besides being the leader of the Aesir, Odin is also the patriarch of the largest family in the Norse pantheon.

Odin's brothers, Vili and Ve, helped him slay Ymir and create the world. Beyond that Norse myth has nothing to say about them. Some sources list the names of Odin's brothers as Hoenir and Lodur, though it's not clear if these are two additional brothers, alternate names for Vili and Ve, or something else. Hoenir, who's described as tall and handsome, makes a minor appearance in a few myths.

Odin's wife is the goddess Frigg. Their children include Baldur the god of peace; Hermod, who rides to Hel to try to ransom the life of his brother Baldur; Hodur the blind god; and according to the *Prose Edda*, Tyr the god of war.

But Odin isn't entirely faithful to Frigg; he's had sons with several other goddesses. By the earth goddess Jord he's the father of Thor. Vidar, who avenges his father's death at Ragnarok by slaying Fenris, and Vali, who avenges Baldur's death, are his sons by the giantesses Grid and Rind, respectively.

The sagas tell us that Odin fathered many mortal heroes. These include Sigi, first of the Volsungs; Skjold, ancestor of the kings of Denmark; Saemingr, ancestor of the Norwegian kings; and Yngvi, forefather of the kings of Sweden.

Odin's Weapons and Talismans

Like many gods throughout world mythology, Odin has some unique possessions that provide him with special powers and abilities.

Gungnir

The first and most important of these is Gungnir ("The Swaying One"), his enchanted spear. It never misses its target, and it automatically returns to his hand after he throws it.

Odin obtained Gungnir thanks to Loki's mischief. One day Loki came upon Thor's wife, Sif, while she slept. Seeing her long, golden hair, a wicked thought came into his head. Taking out his knife he cut all her hair off.

When Thor discovered what had happened to Sif, he knew instantly who was to blame. He wanted to kill Loki, but Odin wouldn't permit it. "None of

Odin rides to war in this work by Arthur Rackham. (PD)

the Aesir may slay another," he said. He decreed that Loki must restore Sif's hair.

Loki journeyed to Svartalfheim and visited some dwarves known to him, the sons of Ivaldi, who possessed wondrous skill with smithcraft. Using all his powers of flattery and persuasion Loki convinced them to make new, living hair for Sif out of purest gold. But he realized that alone wouldn't allay the wrath of the Aesir; he needed more gifts. So he talked the sons of Ivaldi into giving him two other wonders they had made, the magic ship *Skidbladnir* and the spear Gungnir. He presented the ship to Frey and the spear to Odin.

Sometimes Odin lends Gungnir to mortal heroes. A tale in the *Poetic Edda* tells how Dag, son of Hogni, sought vengeance for his father's death at Helgi's hand. He sacrificed to Odin and beseeched the All-Father for help. Odin lent him his spear, and with it Dag slew Helgi.

Draupnir

After regaining the Aesir's favor, Loki bragged about the unmatched skill of his "friends," the sons of Ivaldi. A dwarf named Brokk heard him and claimed that his brother Sindri was a better smith than the sons of Ivaldi. Their argument became so heated that Loki bet his head that Brokk and his brother could not produce greater gifts.

Brokk hurried to Sindri's forge, where despite Loki's interference Sindri made three things. The first was the shining, flying golden boar Gullinbursti. The second was Draupnir ("The Dripper"), an arm-ring that drops from itself eight rings of the same shape and weight every ninth night. The third was the mighty thunderbolt hammer Mjolnir.

Brokk returned to Asgard. He gave Gullinbursti to Frey. Odin received Draupnir, and thus always had rich rewards to give to his followers – a particularly appropriate gift for the All-Father, since generosity was one of the qualities the Norse most valued in a leader. Mjolnir went to Thor, and the Aesir judged it a greater gift than all the others combined. With his typical cunning, Loki weaseled out of his bet by claiming he'd only wagered his head, so Brokk had no right to touch his neck. Brokk settled for sewing Loki's lips together with a leather thong.

Hlidskjalf

Odin also possesses a magic throne called the *Hlidskjalf*, which he keeps in the top room of the tallest tower in his hall Valaskjalf. Anyone who sits in it can see throughout the Nine Worlds, and Odin often sits there so he can learn what takes place in the realms beyond Asgard. Occasionally Frigg sits there too.

The *Poetic Edda* tells how Frey dared to sit on the Hlidskjalf one day and paid for his presumption. In Jotunheim he saw the beautiful giantess Gerd and fell instantly in love. He gave his servant Skirnir his magic sword and his horse to go win her for him, which Skirnir did. But without his sword, Frey was easy prey for Surtur at Ragnarok.

Odin's Animals

Odin has several animal companions.

Sleipnir

Sleipnir ("Sliding One") is Odin's eight-legged steed with magic runes carved on his teeth. The swiftest of all horses, Sleipnir can run over the land or through the sky with equal ease.

OPPOSITE
Odin and his brothers battle the giant Ymir.

Sleipnir is another gift Odin received as a result of Loki's trickery. After the Aesir–Vanir war the Aesir wanted to have a strong wall built around their realm. A smith (actually a giant in disguise) offered to do the job for a high price – Freya, the Sun, and the Moon. Loki convinced the Aesir to accept the offer under the condition that the smith had to complete the job in only three seasons. The smith agreed and immediately went to work. When the gods realized the smith would succeed, they forced Loki to take care of the problem. Realizing the giant's true advantage was his intelligent horse, Svadilfari, Loki changed shape into a beautiful mare. He seductively lured Svadilfari away so the giant couldn't finish building the wall in time. Some months later Loki returned to Asgard with an eight-legged foal at his side and made a present of him to Odin.

Some scholars believe Sleipnir's eight legs represent four pallbearers, and thus emphasize Odin's role as god of the dead. Others have suggested that depictions of eight-legged horses in art may simply represent a horse running swiftly, and that the myth grew out of this.

Hugin and Munin

Odin has two ravens: Hugin ("Thought") and Munin ("Memory"). Every morning they leave Asgard and "fly over all the world" to observe what occurs. In the evening they return, perch on Odin's shoulders, and whisper what they've learned to him.

Freki and Geri

Odin also has two fierce wolves, Freki and Geri (both meaning "The Greedy One"). They lie at his feet when he sits on the Hlidskjalf and when he presides over the feast table in Valhalla.

Valhalla

In addition to Valaskjalf, Odin possesses another hall lauded in song and story – Valhalla, the "Hall of the Slain." Located in a part of Asgard called Gladsheim ("Shining Home") next to the golden-leafed forest Glasir, it's enormous. It has 540 doors, each of them wide enough that 800 warriors can march through shoulder to shoulder. The tables inside are so long they always have room for more feasters. Spears hold up Valhalla's roof, which is thatched with shields. Coats of mail cover the benches; weapons and helmets hang on the walls as decoration.

Two animals wait to greet those who come to Valhalla – a wolf who sits before the western doors, and an eagle who hovers above the hall. Two more live on top of it. One is the goat Heidrun, who grazes on the leaves of a tree named Laeradr (which is part of Yggdrasil). Mead drips from her udders in an endless stream so that those who dwell in Odin's hall always have enough to drink. The other is a deer, Eikthyrnir, from whose antlers water drips down to

WODEN

Anglo-Saxon and Germanic myth features the god *Woden* (sometimes written Wodan, Wotan, Godan), from whom the day-name "Wednesday" (Woden's Day") and numerous English and European place-names derive. Historians know relatively little about him or his worship; what evidence exists mainly takes the form of brief mentions in medieval texts. Most modern scholars conflate him with Odin to a greater or lesser degree, though some argue that the two are distinct deities.

The Anglo-Saxons regarded Woden as a forefather of their kings. They also seem to have considered him a psychopomp, though it's unclear whether their Woden had an equivalent of Valhalla or the valkyries. His name may derive from root words relating to fury, madness, inspiration, or possession, indicating a shamanic link or connection to warfare. Some researchers suspect he may have once been a less important god who gradually took over the functions of Tiwaz (Tyr), thus becoming chief of the gods. Later Christian writers, such as Bede, euhemerized him as a powerful king and royal ancestor. The Nine Herbs Charm, a spell to counteract poison written down in the tenth century, describes Woden "[taking] nine glory-twigs" and smiting a serpent into nine parts. This is reminiscent of Odin glimpsing the mystic runes as he hangs on Yggdrasil.

Medieval folklore described Woden as the leader of the Wild Hunt (sometimes known as Woden's Hunt). Some authorities also see Woden as the root figure behind Father Christmas/Santa Claus.

Hvergelmir, the spring beneath Yggdrasil which is the source of all the rivers in the world.

But the warriors in Valhalla don't subsist on mead alone. For food Odin's "guests" eat the pork of the great boar Saehrímnir. Each day the cook Audhrímnir slaughters the boar and cooks his meat in a cauldron called Eldhrímnir. Odin doesn't eat the pork; he feeds his share to Freki and Geri and subsists only on wine.

The Einherjar

Valhalla is the home of the *einherjar* ("Those Who Fight Alone"), human heroes and warriors chosen to fight for the Aesir. Every day they form armies and battle one another to the death to keep themselves in fighting trim. At day's end they come back to life, hale and whole, and return to Valhalla to drink mead and eat pork.

The Valkyries

Serving Odin and his warriors in Valhalla are the *Valkyries*, the "Choosers of the Slain." These bold, beautiful, lethally-skilled warrior-women follow Odin into battle and select the heroes who will serve the All-Father in the afterlife and fight for the gods at Ragnarok. They also wait upon those warriors in Valhalla, bringing them food and drink.

Some sources list 13 valkyries: Geirahod; Goll; Herfjotur; Hildr; Hlokk; Hrist; Mist; Radgríd; Randgríd; Reginleif; Skeggjold; Skogul;

and Thrudr (Thor's daughter). But other tales mention additional Valkyries by name, calling the exact number into question. These include Brynhildr (the fallen valkyrie who plays a prominent role in the story of Sigurd), Geirskogul, Gondul, Gunnr, and Skuld.

A Valkyrie, by ªRU-MOR.

ODIN: THE MYTHS

Other than his son Thor, and perhaps the mischievous Loki, Odin appears in more Norse myths than any other god. In some, such as the story of the contest between Loki and Brokk, he plays only a minor role at best – typically that of a ruler rendering judgment. But in many he takes center stage.

The Creation of the World

In the beginning only three places existed. In the south was Muspelheim, a world of fire and searing heat; in the north Niflheim, a world of frost and deadly cold; and between them Ginnungagap, the Yawning Chasm, a grassless void. From the spring Hvergelmir in Niflheim the Elivagar rivers poured forth into Ginnungagap, where they froze. The fire and heat from Muspelheim, meeting this poisonous ice, melted it into a thick mist.

Time passed. Then within the mists two beings formed. One was Ymir, an enormous, fierce frost giant; the other Audhumla, a gigantic, hornless cow. The milk from Audhumla's udders provided Ymir with the nourishment he needed to grow even larger and more terrifying.

For a long time Ymir and Audhumla were the only two beings in Ginnungagap. One day Ymir fell into a deep sleep, and while he slept the heat of his body brought forth new life. From his left armpit a male and female jotun emerged, and from the sweat between his legs came a six-headed troll. Soon these horrid beings reproduced, populating the Yawning Chasm with their wild, raucous offspring.

But Ymir wasn't the only one who could create life. Audhumla fed herself by licking the salty frost that formed on the rim of Ginnungagap. From the touch of her tongue and breath a face and body began to take shape in the ice, but her "child" wasn't the same as the ugly spawn of Ymir. Handsome and noble-looking, he was Buri, the first god, and after three days he stepped from the ice fully formed.

The young Odin before sacrificing his youth and vitality in his quest for wisdom. By aRU-MOR.

23

Ymir the Giant, by ªRU-MOR.

Buri had a son, Bor. When Bor came of age he married Bestla, daughter of the giant Bolthorn, and they had three sons: Odin, Vili, and Ve.

The young gods and Ymir did not get along. Eventually Odin, Vili, and Ve fought Ymir, and after a long, fierce battle they slew him. So much blood poured forth from the frost giant's wounds that it drowned all of Ymir's monstrous "children" except the giant Bergelmir and his wife. They climbed on a wooden box and floated away. All the jotuns and trolls of Jotunheim descend from them.

Odin, Vili, and Ve took Ymir's gargantuan body and flung it into Ginnungagap, thus filling the Yawning Chasm and creating Midgard. From his bones and teeth they made the mountains and stones, from his hair the forests, and from the remainder of his blood the rivers and seas. With his eyebrows they built a fence around the wonderful new land to shield it from the attacks of jotuns and other monsters. Lastly they took his skull and set it above Midgard to form the dome of the sky, and Ymir's brains became the clouds.

Odin's brother, Ve, by ªRU-MOR.

As beautiful as it was, the gods' new world had no light. So they took some Muspelheim sparks and placed them in the sky as the stars. Then they got more flame from Muspelheim and used it to create Sol, the sun, and Mani, the moon. They placed each of them in a cart. To the sun's cart Odin hitched the horse Skinfaxe ("Shining Mane"), with bellows at his shoulders to blow cool air over his rear legs so Sol wouldn't burn them. Then he hitched Hrimfaxe ("Frosty Mane") to Mani's cart. In Jotunheim he found the good giantess Nat ("Night") and her son Dag ("Day") to drive Mani and Sol around the sky.

But the rest of the giants preferred darkness and gloom; the bright lights in the sky hurt their eyes. So a jotun named Skoll changed shape into an enormous wolf and began chasing Sol around the sky to eat her, and his brother Hati followed suit and pursued Mani.

The Creation of Man

Odin, Vili, and Ve looked out upon their creation and marveled at it, but also realized how empty it seemed, so they decided to people it. First they created beasts to fill the forests, fish to swim in the waters, and birds to fly through the sky.

Then they took the maggots from Ymir's corpse and fashioned them into the *Dvergar*, or dwarves, short, ugly little beings to live deep underground in the realm of Svartalfheim. They soon learned just how irascible, distrustful, greedy, and temperamental the dwarves could be, but also that they possessed

Odin's brother, Vili, by aRU-MOR.

their own sort of wisdom and a matchless skill at creating things. Thanks to the dwarves, the Aesir never lacked for gold, silver, or fine weapons and possessions.

Next Odin and his brothers considered what form humans, their worshippers and the main inhabitants of Midgard, should take. While walking along the shore they came upon an ash tree and an alder that they thought would make good material for creating the first humans. Odin gave the two trees souls, Vili granted them intelligence and willpower, and finally Ve breathed warmth, senses, and emotions into them. The trees twisted, turned, transformed, and at last came to life in human shape as the first man and woman, Ask ("Ash") and Embla ("Alder"). Their descendants became all the men and women who peopled the wide world.

Odin Seeks Wisdom

Several Norse myths address Odin's quest for wisdom and knowledge, particularly pertaining to Ragnarok and to mystic subjects. In fact, some experts view the desire for knowledge and supernatural lore as the personality trait that best defines Odin.

In many cases Odin obtains wisdom through deception. Disguised as a wanderer, and using names whose meanings often hint at his true nature and purpose, he speaks with giants and men to learn what he needs to know. Those he interacts with don't realize who he is until it's too late.

Odin Hangs From Yggdrasil

The earliest wisdom story in the Norse myth-cycle tells how Odin sacrificed himself to himself in search of greater insight. At the end of nine days and nights of hanging from one of Yggdrasil's branches, starving and in pain, he gazed down and perceived the runes, which gods and men could use both for writing and to perform magic. In the words of the *Poetic Edda*:

I ween that I hung on the windy tree,
Hung there for nights full nine;
With the spear I was wounded, and offered I was
To Odin, myself to myself,
On the tree that none may ever know
What root beneath it runs.
None made me happy with loaf or horn,

And there below I looked;
I took up the runes, shrieking I took them,
And forthwith back I fell.

That is how Yggdrasil got its name – "Ygg's (Odin's) Horse," meaning both a gallows and the means by which Odin travels to other realms and gains knowledge. It's also how Odin earned many of his names (such as Hangagud, "God of the Hanged"). But some aspects of Odin's ordeal remain unclear. Hanging by the neck is the image that most readily comes to mind, and in some respects makes the most sense. But Norse art features some depictions of Christ hung with his arms amid tangled branches, suggesting that the Odin self-sacrifice story may already have planted such an image in the Norse mind. Jere Fleck has argued in favor of an interpretation that Odin hung upside down, by his feet, and thus could literally "take up" the runes from the ground and then be "reborn" like a baby emerging from the womb. Others suggest Odin hung from the part of Yggdrasil that's in the underworld, a place that's frequently a source of knowledge for the All-Father.

Odin sacrifices himself to himself in this early 20th-century illustration by W.G. Collingwood. (PD)

The nature of Odin's self-sacrifice – hanging from a tree, wounded with a spear – invites comparison to the crucifixion of Jesus Christ in the Bible, which figuratively refers to the cross as a "tree." Some scholars have seized upon this to argue that the myth indicates an adoption of Christian stories and motifs into the Norse mythos. But as others have pointed out, this form of sacrifice is known from Norse and other early cultures, and is even referenced elsewhere in Norse literature (such as Starkad's sacrifice of King Vikar). Therefore it seems more likely that Odin's self-sacrifice attempts to explain the origin of this practice and/or to provide a mythical representation of a sort of shamanic initiation into sacred lore.

Odin Drinks From Mimir's Well

Odin also gained wisdom from the jotun Mimir. Unlike many giants, Mimir wasn't crude and brutal, but wise and learned. He owned Mimir's Well, which sprang from the ground where one of Yggdrasil's roots emerged in Jotunheim. Anyone who drank from the Well earned wisdom, but first they had to pay whatever price Mimir asked.

Undaunted by the stories he had heard, Odin rode to Mimir's steading.

"I seek a draught from your Well," he told the wise jotun. "What price will you take for it?"

Odin, after offering his eye for wisdom, by ᵃRU-MOR.

"Your left eye, o' All-Father, is the price I must have for a drink from my Well. No one else has ever dared to pay my price. Will you?"

Odin shuddered and began to turn away, but then he thought of all he had seen from his high seat the Hlidskjalf – the giants of Jotunheim, eager to destroy gods and men; the terrors lurking in Niflheim; Surtur and his fearsome horde of fire giants and Ragnarok that was to come. His need for knowledge and insight bolstered his courage, and he replied, "I will."

"Drink, then," Mimir said, drawing a horn-full of water from the Well. Odin drained the horn, marveling at the new wisdom that came to him as he did so. Then without complaint or groan of pain he raised his hand to his face, plucked out his left eye, and gave it to Mimir. Mimir dropped it into the Well, and ever after he could see through it whatever Odin saw.

Odin's relationship with Mimir continued in an unusual way. After the Aesir made peace with the Vanir, Odin sent Hoenir to them as hostage. Knowing his brother wasn't very bright or decisive, the All-Father asked Mimir to accompany him. Impressed by Hoenir's appearance, lineage, and charm, the Vanir made him a chieftain. But they soon learned that he always followed Mimir's advice. If the wise jotun wasn't in the council hall Hoenir responded to every dispute by saying, "Let others decide." Realizing the Aesir had given them a poor hostage, but not daring to take revenge by harming mighty Odin's brother, the Vanir chopped off Mimir's head and sent it to the All-Father. Using his magic Odin brought Mimir's head back to life, and ever after he sought counsel from Mimir in times of need.

❧·❧·❧·❧·❧·❧

The *Prose Edda* relates a different tale. It says that when Ragnarok begins, Odin rides to Mimir's Well to seek the wise jotun's counsel. Regardless of which story is "correct," the essential fact – that Odin seeks Mimir's advice in difficult situations – remains true.

Some mythologists speculate that Mimir may be the unnamed brother of Bestla (Odin's mother) referred to in the *Poetic Edda*. That would make Odin Mimir's nephew, though their interaction in the myths shows no sign of familial affection.

The Wisdom Contest With Vafthrudnir

Mimir isn't the only jotun from whom Odin sought lore. The *Vafthrudnismal*, the third section of the *Poetic Edda*, tells the story of Odin's wisdom contest with Vafthrudnir.

Despite the wisdom he had already gained, Odin remained eager for greater perspicacity, especially regarding Ragnarok. One day he said to Frigg, "I intend to go to Jotunheim to match wits with Vafthrudnir to see what I can learn."

"It would be better if you stayed home," Frigg said. "Vafthrudnir is the wisest of the giants, and cruel to contend with." But her warning did not dissuade him, and, putting on a disguise, to the land of the jotuns he went.

He entered Vafthrudnir's hall, where the giant and his companions caroused, and presented himself as one who sought hospitality.

"Who is it that enters my hall?" Vafthrudnir asked. "You have to be full of wisdom if you're to walk away from here!"

"I am Gagnradr," Odin said, concealing his identity with a false name, "and I have come to see which one of us is the wisest, o' Giant."

Vafthrudnir laughed long and loud. "Good! I like a bold challenge. Take a seat in my hall."

Odin remained standing. "A poor man who visits a rich man should be sparing of speech, or be silent."

"As you wish. Tell me, then, the names of the horses who pull the Sun and the Moon across the sky."

"They are Skinfaxe and Hrímfaxe, Shining-Mane and Frost-Mane."

That surprised Vafthrudnir, for most men and giants lacked that lore. So he asked a harder question. "What is the name of the river that divides Asgard from Jotunheim?"

"Ifing is that river, which flows deep and swift, yet never freezes no matter how cold it becomes."

"What is the name of the plain where Surtur, king of the fire giants, will meet the gods in battle at Ragnarok?"

"Vigrid, the plain that spreads a hundred leagues in all directions," Odin answered to the giant's astonishment.

"You've proven your wisdom, Gagnradr. Come, have a seat at my bench! Let us speak together and match our lore. But we play for hard stakes here. We'll wager our heads on whose wisdom is the greater."

"So be it," said Odin. "Tell me first, from where did the earth and sky come?"

Vafthrudnir answered right away. "The gods made the earth from Ymir's flesh, the rocks from his bones, the sea from his blood, and the sky from his skull."

"And where did the Moon and Sun come from?"

"Mundilfari is the name of the father of both Sol and Mani," Vafthrudnir replied.

"And what about Day and Night?"

"Delling is father of Day, and Nor of Night."

Odin continued. "From where do Winter and Summer come?"

"Vindsval fathered cruel Winter, and Svasuth bountiful Summer."

Next Odin asked, "Who was the oldest of the Aesir or of Ymir's kin in days long past?"

"Aurgelmir, father of Thrudgelmir father of Bergelmir."

"And from where did Aurgelmir come, wisest of giants?"

"Venom-drops spurted from Elivagar, and in Ginnungagap they grew to create him."

"And how did Aurgelmir have children, since he had no she-giant?"

"As he slept a male and female jotun grew under his armpits, and a six-headed son from between his shanks."

"And what of you, Vafthrudnir – what's the first thing you remember?"

"So old am I that my earliest memory is of Bergelmir in his cradle."

"From where comes the wind, that men never see?" asked Odin"

At the edge of the world sits Hraesvelgr, a giant in eagle's shape, and with the beating of his wings he creates the wind," Vafthrudnir replied.

"Since you're so wise, now tell me from whence Njord, a god who rules temples by the hundreds, came among the Aesir?"

"The sea-god was born in Vanaheim among the Vanir, and came to Asgard as hostage for his people. After the fall of the gods he will return home to Vanaheim."

"In what enclosure do ever-living warriors slay one another with swords, then fare forth from the battlefield to drain goblets together in good fellowship?"

"The einherjar in Odin's garth ride in from the fray to sit settled once more."

"Of all the secrets of the gods and giants you speak the whole truth, Vafthrudnir! So tell me, who among men will survive the Fimbulwinter?"

"Lif and Lifthrasir they are called, who will hide in Hoddmimir's Wood and live on the morning dew. From them shall spring a new race of men."

"And how will there be light for this new race of men after Fenris swallows the Sun?"

"Before the wolf swallows her the Sun shall give birth to a daughter, her equal in glory, who shall take her place in the sky."

"Who are those maidens who fare swiftly over the sea, traveling with the wisdom of the mind?"

"They are three throngs of maidens, the daughters of giants, who journey to homes in Midgard to assist with the birth of children."

"After Ragnarok, when Surtur's fires have died away, what gods will remain to govern the effects of the Aesir?"

"Vidar and Vali the sons of Odin will live in the gods' temples, and Modi and Magni the sons of Thor shall have Mjolnir."

THE RUNES

The runes referred to in the myth of Odin's self-sacrifice are a form of writing that evolved for the Germanic languages early in the first millennium AD. Historians believe they may have derived from the Old Italic alphabets that Germanic mercenaries fighting for the Romans would have been exposed to. The Scandinavian forms of the runes are often known as *Futhark* based on the first six letters of the runic alphabet.

The runes, which were used both to write with ink and to carve in stone and wood, developed into various forms over time. The earliest, *Elder Futhark* (second to eighth centuries), featured 24 letters. Each probably had a name based on the sound it represented, but if so these names aren't recorded; scholars have attempted to reconstruct them from Proto-Germanic. The Anglo-Saxon or Anglo-Frisian forms of the runes, used in the fifth to 11th centuries and featuring 29–33 characters, have known names listed in the Old English Rune Poem from the eighth or ninth century. As Proto-Norse transformed into Old Norse, the Elder Futhark became the *Younger Futhark*, a simpler 16-character alphabet used from the ninth to 11th centuries. It came in two forms, a long-branch version used in Denmark, and a short-branch version found in Sweden and Norway.

From the 12th to the 15th centuries, a medieval form of the runes developed that expanded Younger Futhark to 27 characters. The medieval runes tend to display a large number of variants across sources.

But the Vikings didn't use the runes just for written communication. They also formed an important part of the Norse mystical tradition. Each rune's name meant

A Viking rune stone from around AD 1000 in Sweden. (Mary Evans Picture Library)

it could represent that thing for occult purposes. For example, a wizard could use the *tiwaz* rune, named for the god Tyr, to call upon the war god for victory in battle. Carving a rune, particularly three times, was a part of many spells. In the *Poetic Edda*, Odin describes his magical power to bring a hanged man back to life:

> A twelfth I know, if high on a tree
> I see a hanged man swing;
> So do I write and color the runes
> That forth he fares,
> And to me talks."

Another well-known example occurs in *Egil's Saga* when Bard offers Egil a horn filled with poisoned drink. Suspecting treachery, Egil cuts the palm of his hand, then carves runes on the horn and smears them with his blood, chanting:

> I carve runes on this horn,
> redden the spell with my blood,
> Wise words I choose for the cup
> wrought from the wild beast's
> ear-roots;
> drink as we wish this mead
> brought by merry servants,
> let us find out how we fare
> from the ale that Bard blessed.

When he has finished, the horn shatters and the poisoned mead spills into the straw on the floor, saving his life.

In the *Poetic Edda*, Sigrdrifa (Brynhildr) describes several forms of rune magic she knows – including "victory runes" to carve on swords, a favorite motif of Fantasy authors and artists ever since.

"And Odin himself – what fate will befall the All-Father in the last battle?"

"The Fenris wolf will swallow him. His son Vidar shall avenge him by tearing the monster's cold jaws asunder."

Having learned what he came to learn, Odin next asked a question he knew Vafthrudnir could not answer. "What were the last words that Odin, the All-Father, whispered into the ear of his son, Baldur, as he lay upon the funeral pyre?"

At that Vafthrudnir stood up from his chair and pointed an accusatory finger at his guest. "Only the All-Father himself could know that, and only he would ask it. You are Odin, and I cannot answer your riddle. My head is forfeit to you, for you are the wisest of beings."

❧ ❧ ❧ ❧ ❧ ❧

In its rhythm of question-and-response Odin's wisdom contest with Vafthrudnir encapsulates the cycle of Norse myth. The giants prove their legitimacy and power by establishing that they came first, possess great lore, and will slay the gods at Ragnarok. But by winning the wisdom contest Odin establishes that ultimately the course of events will sweep the giants aside so that the surviving gods and men may live in peace. The lay also follows a pattern common to many Norse myths, in which the gods take things from the giants but lose nothing in return. Some mythologists even see the contest as having paternal overtones, with Odin triumphing over his ancestors and claiming their power in much the same way that Zeus defeated Kronos and drove him out of heaven.

The Magic Mead

A beautiful goddess named Gullveig, one of the Vanir, came to Asgard. A sorceress who was "in magic wise," she disturbed the Aesir. They pierced her with spears, and in Odin's hall they burned her. She arose, alive and unharmed, from the flames. Three times they cast her into the fire, and three times she lived. After that her name became Heidr, and she bewitched minds and aided the schemes of evil women.

Odin and the gods met in council to decide whether they should pay "tribute" to the Vanir to buy peace, and whether all gods (both Aesir and Vanir) or only the Aesir should partake in the "feast" of sacrifices offered up by men. Odin decided in favor of the Aesir. He hurled his spear over the host of the Vanir, and thus the Aesir–Vanir war, the first war in all the world, began. Both sides fought long and fiercely; the Vanir broke the wall that protected Asgard and trampled the plain. But strive as they might the Vanir could not overcome the mighty Aesir, and so the two sides agreed to make peace.

To seal their truce the gods did two things. First, they exchanged hostages. Njord, Frey, and Freya came to Asgard, while Hoenir and Mimir went to live in Vanaheim. Secondly, all the gods gathered around a huge cauldron. They chewed up special herbs, roots, and berries and spat them into the cauldron, filling it with a thick liquid. They agreed to keep this liquid as a symbol of their truce. From it arose Kvasir, a spirit of great wisdom who would provide sage counsel to both groups of gods.

Unfortunately the gods didn't have the advantage of Kvasir's knowledge for very long. Two dwarves, Galarr and Fjalarr, murdered him and took his blood to Svartalfheim. There they mixed it with honey and magic herbs and brewed Odroerir, the magic mead. Anyone who drank the mead would become a poet, charmingly eloquent and able to recite beautiful verse at will.

The two evil dwarves traveled to Jotunheim. There they found a simple-minded giant named Gilling, whom they persuaded to row them out to sea. Knowing Gilling couldn't swim, Galarr and Fjalarr steered the boat onto the rocks. They floated on the

Odin, in the form of an eagle, stealing the Mead of Poetry, from an 18th-century Icelandic manuscript. (PD)

pieces of the boat and laughed as Gilling drowned. When they returned to shore they went to Gilling's house and asked his wife if she wanted to see where he drowned. When she came outside they killed her, too, by dropping a millstone on her.

Fjalarr and Galarr continued their cruel mischief wherever and whenever they could, and with their powers of verse they composed songs praising themselves for their evil deeds. But then Gilling's son Suttung tracked them down. Strong and cunning, he caught the two dwarves and put them on a rock that the tide would cover so he could watch them suffer and die.

As the water rose higher and higher, Galarr and Fjalarr begged Suttung to take them back to land. They offered him gold, and he laughed at them. They offered him gems and jewelry as beautiful as Freya's necklace Brisingamen, and still he laughed. At last in desperation they offered him Odroerir.

That caught Suttung's interest. He let Galarr and Fjalarr keep their lives in exchange for the mead of poetry. He poured Odroerir into three cauldrons that he hid inside the mountain Hnitbjorg. He put his beautiful daughter Gunnlod inside the mountain to watch over the mead.

Word reached Odin of the death of Kvasir, and he grieved. To punish the dwarves who murdered Kvasir he sealed them in their caves in Svartalfheim, forbidding them to ever come to Midgard, Jotunheim, or Asgard again. From them he learned of Odroerir, and he determined to win it for the gods.

Suttung had a brother, Baugi, who farmed a large amount of land with the help of nine thralls. Odin, in disguise and using the name Bolverk

An early 20th-century depiction of Odin stealing the Mead of Poetry. (PD)

OPPOSITE
Odin sacrifices himself to himself by hanging from the branches of Yggdrasil.

("Evil Work"), came among the thralls while they mowed hay with their scythes. He asked if they wanted their scythes sharpened, and they said yes. He took a whetstone from his belt pouch and sharpened the scythes so well that they cut hay better than ever. All of the thralls clamored to buy the whetstone, but rather than sell it Odin threw it among them. As they struggled for it they cut each other's throats with their scythes.

Odin obtained hospitality that night from Baugi. The giant complained of the loss of his thralls, saying, "Without men to work my fields I shall have no hay to feed my livestock during the winter."

"I can work your fields for you," Odin said.

"The work of one man is not enough. I need nine men, so wide are my fields."

"I can do the work of nine men," Odin said, "if you can pay me with a drink of Odroerir, the magic mead."

"The mead belongs to my brother Suttung; I have no control over it. But if you work for me I'll go with you to ask him for a drink."

Odin agreed to this. He worked for Baugi the rest of the season, easily doing the work of nine men. At the end of that time the two of them went to Suttung to beg a drink of the magic mead for Bolverk, but Suttung refused.

When they returned to Baugi's home Odin said, "You must keep your side of our bargain and help me get my reward. Come with me." He led Baugi to Hnitbjorg. He produced an auger, and said, "Use this to drill a hole into the mountain."

Baugi drilled and drilled, then claimed to have finished. Odin blew into the hole and stone dust flew back in his face. From this he knew Baugi had tried to trick him, so he told the giant to keep working. At last Baugi bored through to the interior of the mountain. Odin changed into a serpent. Baugi tried to stab him with the auger but Odin moved too quickly for him and slipped into the mountain unharmed.

Inside Odin found Gunnlod guarding the three mead-filled cauldrons.

"Come no closer!" she warned. "If you do I will spill the magic mead."

Odin resumed his true form – a tall, handsome god – and spoke in soothing tones. "Gunnlod, Gunnlod!" he said. "Do you wish to remain

THE UNKNOWN ADVENTURES OF ODIN

The *Poetic Edda* mentions several adventures of Odin's which have unfortunately been lost to modern readers. They include:

• taking on the identity of Jalk in Asmund's hall for some reason

• taking on the identity of Kjalar in an incident that involved drawing a hand sled

• using the names Svithur and Svithrir in the hall or domain of one Sokkmimir, when he tricked the "old giant" and singlehandedly slew the son of the mighty giant Midvitnir

• spending five winters with Fjolvar on Algroen Island, where together they fought fierce wars, performed great deeds, and had their choice of women

• confronting a hardy giant named Hlebard (who gave him a magic staff or wand) and "[stealing] his wits away."

• failing to seduce "Billing's daughter," a clever woman who told him to come back later and then put a female dog in her bed

here forever?" Three nights he stayed with Gunnlod, and she told him he could have one drink of mead for each night. With three great gulps he drank all the mead. Then he changed into the form of an eagle and flew toward Asgard, abandoning the giantess who had helped him.

Suttung saw the eagle leave Hnitbjorg and realized what had happened. He took the form of an eagle himself and pursued Odin. The All-Father was so full of mead that he couldn't fly swiftly, so Suttung gained on him.

Heimdall saw the two birds approaching the ramparts of Asgard and deduced who they were. He alerted the Aesir and told them to place all their cauldrons, kettles, and pots near the wall. Odin had just enough time to spit out the mead and make it safely inside Asgard before Suttung caught up to him. The hapless giant had to return to Jotunheim empty-handed.

After that adventure Odin spoke even more eloquently than before and often in verse. At times he would reward gods and men he favored with a sip of the wondrous mead, and they, too, became great bards.

Odin Gives Wisdom To Men

Odin didn't keep his wisdom to himself as if it were a dragon's hoard. He shared it not only with the other gods but with his human worshippers in Midgard. One of the most intriguing parts of the *Poetic Edda* is the *Havamal*, "the Sayings of Har" (Har, "High," being one of Odin's names). The longest part of the *Edda*, it consists mostly of advice and aphorisms spoken by Odin. Much of Odin's wisdom is genuine and noble, and even told with a touch of humor at times. On the other hand, the second section of the Sayings takes a different tone – it provides cynical, bitter advice about women.

Here are some examples of Odin's counsel to mortals:

Within the gates ere a man shall go,
Full warily let him watch,
Full long let him look about him;
For little he knows where a foe may lurk,
And sit in the seats within.

Fire he needs who with frozen knees
Has come from the cold without;
Food and clothes must the farer have,
The man from the mountains come.

The foolish man for friends all those
Who laugh at him will hold;
When among the wise he marks it not
Though hatred of him they speak.

Better a house, though a hut it be,
A man is master at home;
A pair of goats and a patched-up roof
Are better far than begging.

Away from his arms in the open field
A man should fare not a foot;
For never he knows when the need for a spear
Shall arise on the distant road.

To his friend a man a friend shall prove,
To him and the friend of his friend;
But never a man shall friendship make
With one of his foeman's friends.

Cattle die, and kinsmen die,
And so one dies one's self;
But a noble name will never die,
If good renown one gets.

A man shall trust not the oath of a maid,
Nor the word a woman speaks;
For their hearts on a whirling wheel were fashioned,
And fickle their breasts were formed.

Odin's Bragging Contest With Thor

One of the most unusual myths featuring Odin is the *Harbarzljod*, or "Lay of

Harbard," in the *Poetic Edda*. This distinctive poem primarily takes the form of a *flyting* or *senna*, a contest of insults, and a *mannjafnadr*, a boasting contest, in which the participants compare deeds and accomplishments, each striving to outdo the other). It features Harbard, a ferryman who most scholars believe is Odin in disguise, debating with Thor, who wants Harbard to ferry him across an inlet as he returns from fighting giants in Jotunheim. Their insults and boasts refer to many other Norse myths. Here are a few examples.

Thor said:

> Thjazi I felled, the giant fierce,
> And I hurled the eyes of Alvaldi's son
> To the heavens hot above;
> Of my deeds the mightiest marks are these,
> That all men since can see.
> What, Harbard, didst thou the while?

Harbard said:

> Much love-craft I wrought with them who ride by night,
> When I stole them by stealth from their husbands;
> A giant hard was Hlebard, methinks:
> His wand he gave me as gift,
> And I stole his wits away.

Thor said:

> Thou didst repay good gifts with evil mind.

Harbard said:

> The oak must have what it shaves from another;
> In such things each for himself.
> What, Thor, didst thou the while?

Thor said:

> Eastward I fared, of the giants I felled
> Their ill-working women who went to the mountain;
> And large were the giants' throng if all were alive;
> No men would there be in Midgard more.
> What, Harbar, didst thou the while?

Harbard said:

> In Valland I was, and wars I raised,
> Princes I angered, and peace brought never;
> The noble who fall in the fight hath Odin,
> And Thor hath the race of the thralls.

Many things about Harbard's Lay remain enigmatic, including Harbard's identity. Some early scholars equated him with Loki, since it would certainly be in character for the mischievous trickster god to harass and insult Thor for fun. But more recent scholarship rejects this idea and fixes firmly on Odin as Harbard's true identity. Not only is "Harbard" one of Odin's alternate names, but the exploits he boasts of – consorting with witches, seducing maidens and giantesses, stirring up warfare among mortals – are just the sorts of things other eddic lays and sagas describe him, and not Loki, doing.

From a narrative perspective, Odin's reasons for delaying and ridiculing Thor are obscure, but the poem's purpose becomes clearer when one considers the social circumstances in which it was created. The composer, a poet and probably either a nobleman or the servant of a nobleman, favors Odin, the god of rulers, warfare, and poetry. Even though Thor's adventures, such as slaying giants and protecting Midgard, have greater worth than Odin's exploits of seducing women and fomenting war, the lay's sympathies rest entirely with the All-Father. In every exchange he gets the better of Thor, who comes across as a fairly dull fellow leading a drab existence.

Some studies view the *Harbarzljod* as reflecting competition between the two gods for worshippers, and in fact several other sources refer to the rivalry between the two cults. For example, in the *Eyrbyggja Saga*, Odin-worshipper Harald Fairhair drives Thor-worshipper Hrolfr Mostrarskegg out of Norway. In the *Flateyjarbok*, King Eric of Sweden prays to Odin for help in battle against Thor-worshipper Styrbiorn the Strong, and Odin provides him with the means to disable and destroy Styrbiorn's army.

"Odin in Torment," by W.G. Collingwood. (PD)

The Story of Agnar and Geirrod

The fourth section of the *Poetic Edda*, the *Grimnismal* or "Lay of Grimnir," also shows Odin in (to modern eyes) a somewhat questionable light. Containing

OPPOSITE
Odin trades his eye for a
drink from Mimir's Well.

both prose and verse sections, it has long caused debate among scholars as to which parts of it are original and which are later additions. The fact that much of the lay is simply Odin reciting cosmological information (facts which later writers could easily insert) only complicates the analysis, but makes *Grimnismal* a valuable source of Norse lore.

Some scholars believe *Grimnismal* parallels the myth of Odin's self-sacrifice – just like when he hung from Yggdrasil, here Odin withstands torment to acquire/demonstrate shamanic knowledge and power. In some respects it also provides an object lesson regarding human conduct toward the Aesir. Geirrod's failure to feed his guest, as mandated by the sacred laws of hospitality, is tantamount to a failure to offer sacrifices and honor to the gods.

 භ · භ · භ · භ · භ · භ

A king, Hraudung, had two sons, Agnar, age ten, and Geirrod, age eight. One day while they were fishing the wind blew them far out to sea. During the night they crashed onto a small island where lived a fisherman and his wife, Odin and Frigg in disguise. They agreed to care for the boys during the winter, and in the spring Odin would build them a new boat so they could return home.

During the winter Odin showed the most favor to the strong, fierce Geirrod. He taught him to hunt and fish, and the arts of war. Agnar also learned these things, but he preferred the company of Frigg, who taught him many things and instilled wisdom in him.

In the spring the boys set out in their new boat. As it approached the shore, Geirrod leaped onto land and shoved the boat with Agnar still in it back out to sea, shouting, "Now go where all trolls may take you!" Agnar drifted helplessly until he reached another land, where he began living with an ogress in a cave. Geirrod returned home, and since Hraudung had died during the winter he became king.

Some years later Odin and Frigg had returned to Asgard and were sitting on Hlidskjalf. Odin said, "Look there, see how your foster son Agnar has to live in a cave, while my foster son Geirrod is a king."

"A poor sort of king he is. He lets his guests starve if too many of them arrive."

"That is untrue!" Odin said. "And to prove it, I will go visit Geirrod."

"Best keep your wits about you, then," Frigg said.

After Odin left she sent her chambermaid Fulla to Geirrod to warn him that a sorcerer intended to bewitch him. Fulla told Geirrod that he could recognize the sorcerer because no dog would run at him.

When a wanderer arrived at Geirrod's castle and the king's vicious dogs ignored him, Geirrod seized him and chained him between two fires. But despite the pain the man told the king only his name, Grimnir ("The Masked One").

Eight nights passed, with cruel Geirrod and his equally cruel men mocking and tormenting Grimnir each night. They fed him nothing, but on the ninth night Geirod's young son, named Agnar after his uncle, brought Grimnir a horn full of beer. He whispered that the king was wrong to so mistreat one who had committed no crime.

As the fire blazed ever closer around him, Grimnir began to sing. First he praised Agnar for his mercy and charity. Then he described the world of the Aesir, their homes in Asgard, and how they made Midgard to protect men. At the very end of the song he revealed his identity:

> Drunk art thou, Geirrod, too much didst thou drink,
> Much hast thou lost, for help no more
> From me or my heroes thou hast.
> Small heed didst thou take to all that I told,
> And false were the words of thy friends;
> For now the sword of my friend I see,
> That waits all wet with blood.
> Thy sword-pierced body shall Ygg have soon,
> For thy life is ended at last;
> The maids are hostile; now Odin behold!
> Now come to me if thou canst!

Geirrod had listened to Grimnir's recitation seated on his throne, with his sword half-drawn from its scabbard lying across his knees. When Odin revealed his true identity, Geirrod stood up from his seat to take the All-Father away from the flames. The sword tumbled from his lap and fell out of the scabbard, striking the floor pommel-first. Just then Geirrod tripped and fell, impaling himself on his own blade and so dying an ignominious death. Odin vanished, and thereafter young Agnar became a wise and just king of that land.

Odin Banishes Loki's Children

Odin learned that Loki had a wife, Angrboda, in Jotunheim, and that together they had three monstrous children. He sent the gods to seize these children and bring them before him.

Loki's first child was the prodigious serpent Jormungandr. Odin took hold of Jormungandr and flung him into the ocean. There he dwelt, growing and growing, until he became so enormous that his body circled the world and he bit into his own tail. Gods and men called him Midgardsormr, the Midgard Serpent.

Loki's second child, Hel, took the form of a woman, but one side of her body was black-skinned living flesh, while the other half was the pallid flesh of a corpse. Odin sent her far away, to the world that came to bear her name, and gave her dominion over all those who died of starvation, disease, or old age.

Loki's third child, most fearsome of all, was the dark-furred wolf Fenris. He remained in Asgard for a time, but Odin realized that the gods had to restrain him. Twice they forged mighty chains and dared Fenris to test himself against them. Both times Fenris easily broke the chains.

In desperation Odin sent Frey's servant Skirnir to Svartalfheim to seek the aid of the dwarves. The dwarves took five things – the sound made by the footfall of a cat, the spittle of a bird, the breath of a fish, hairs from a woman's beard, and the roots of stones – and wrapped them around the sinews of a bear to create Gleipnir. It resembled a silken ribbon, but not even Thor had the strength to break it.

The Aesir dared Fenris to try to break Gleipnir, but the dread wolf suspected treachery.

"I think this ribbon is a thing of sorcery, and so I will not be able to break it," he said. But he knew that if he succeeded the fame of his strength would spread throughout the Nine Worlds, so he asked, "If I let you put it on me, will you take it off if I cannot break it?"

"We will," said Odin.

"One of you must place his hand within my jaws as surety that you will keep your promise, and I will let you bind me."

A 1906 illustration of Odin casting Loki's children out of Asgard. (PD)

Of all the Aesir only Tyr was brave and selfless enough to put his sword-hand between the wolf's jaws. After he did, the Aesir bound Fenris, and when Gleipnir held firm against his vast strength Odin forswore himself and refused to take it off. In his rage Fenris bit off Tyr's hand at the wrist.

Baldur's Dream

The events leading up to the most tragic tale in Norse mythology, the death of Baldur, began with Odin's efforts to protect his son as described in *Baldrs draumr* ("Baldur's Dream"), a short lay in the *Poetic Edda*. It contains no significant new mythological information, but its details provide a grim flavor to the events described in the *Voluspa*.

ര‌ഗ•ര‌ഗ•ര‌ഗ•ര‌ഗ•ര‌ഗ•ര‌ഗ

Baldur, the most beloved of the gods, was having dark, disturbing dreams. The Aesir met in council to decide what this might mean. Odin declared that he would travel to the grave of a volva and seek answers from her. He saddled Sleipnir and rode toward Hel. As he neared that dreadful place he passed a fearsome dog with blood spattered on its chest, Garm, the hound of Hel.

The burial mound of the volva stood just outside the eastern gate of Hel. Using his necromantic arts Odin summoned her from the dead, and her spirit rose, groaning, from its grave.

> What is the man, to me unknown,
> That has made me travel the troublous road?

I was snowed on with snow, and smitten with rain,
And drenched with dew; long was I dead.

Odin replied.

Vegtam my name, I am Valtam's son;
Speak thou of Hel, for of heaven I know:
For whom are the benches bright with rings,
And the platforms gay bedecked with gold?
The shade of the wise woman said,
Here for Baldr the mead is brewed,
The shining drink, and a shield lies o'er it;
But their hope is gone from the mighty gods.
Unwilling I spake, and now would be still.

Under further questioning the volva revealed more, including that Hodur would slay Baldur and Vali would avenge one brother by slaying the other. But at last she realized to whom she spoke.

Vegtam thou art not, as erstwhile I thought;
Odin thou art, the enchanter old.

Odin replied.

No wise-woman art thou, nor wisdom hast;
Of giants three the mother art thou.
Finally, the woman said,
Home ride, Odin, be ever proud;
For no one of men shall seek me more
Till Loki wanders loose from his bonds,
And to the last strife the destroyers come.

A statue of Loki tricking Hodur into killing Baldur. (Ivy Close Images / Alamy)

The Death of Baldur

Frigg sought to protect Baldur by getting everything in the Nine Worlds, living and unliving, to swear never to harm him. Assured of Baldur's safety, the Aesir gathered around him and amused themselves by hurling weapons and other dangerous things at him, only to watch them cause no injury and drop to the ground. But Loki learned from Frigg that she had elicited no promise from the mistletoe. He carved a dart from mistletoe wood and gave it to the blind god Hodur, who threw it at his brother. Pierced through the heart, Baldur fell dead.

Hermod rides to hell to try and free Baldur. (Ivy Close Images / Alamy)

Baldur's brother Hermod rode Sleipnir to the underworld. There Hel promised him that if everything in the world, living and unliving, would weep for Baldur, she would release him. The Aesir sent messengers throughout the world, and all things wept for love of Baldur – all but one. In a cave one of the messengers found a giantess named Thokk, who was Loki in disguise. She refused to weep, saying "Let Hel keep what she has."

And so Baldur remained dead.

The Binding of Loki

Some time after Baldur's death, the sea giant Aegir threw a feast for the Aesir. After Loki killed Aegir's servant Fimafeng in a fit of jealousy, the other gods drove him away. But he soon returned and began exchanging bitter insults with each of the gods, sparing none of them the lash of his tongue. At last he made them so angry they called on Thor, who instantly appeared. Loki insulted him too and then fled in fear of his life.

The malicious god hid from the Aesir, but they found him and caught him. At Odin's command they used the entrails of his son Narfi to tie him to three flat stones. Vengeful Skadi put a venomous serpent above him to drip poison on his face. After that Loki's wife Sigyn always stood next to him with a bowl to catch the poison. Whenever she had to empty it and the serpent's venom dripped onto Loki his agonized struggles caused earthquakes in Midgard.

Ragnarok, the Doom of the Gods

All things must come to an end, even the gods. But unlike most mythologies, Norse myth describes in detail how this apocalyptic event – *Ragnarok* ("The Final Destiny Of The Gods") – occurs.

ಌ·ಌ·ಌ·ಌ·ಌ·ಌ

Things grew worse and worse in the Nine Worlds, and in Midgard men warred ceaselessly among themselves. Then came the *Fimbulwinter*, three years without anything but icy winds, driving snow, and widespread starvation. So great were the numbers of the dead that both Valhalla and Hel's hall nearly ran out of room.

Finally the roosters of Jotunheim, Asgard, and Hel crowed, signaling that the end approached. The Norns ceased spinning the threads of fate; Yggdrasil shuddered from root to crown and dropped all its leaves. Garm, the hound of Hel, bayed, and the sound echoed throughout the Nine Worlds. All bonds loosened; both Fenris and his father Loki went free at last.

Heimdall, the watchman of the gods, looked out and saw all the foes of the Aesir marching toward Asgard. From the east came the vast host of giants from Jotunheim. Dread spirits from Hel accompanied them in the Naglfar, an enormous ship captained by Loki that was made from the nails of dead men. From the south came Surtur and the fire giants of Muspelheim. Most terrifying of all were Fenris, whose gaping jaws scraped the ground below and sky above, and his brother Jormungandr, who flooded the world as he heaved his vast bulk out of the ocean.

Heimdall blew the Gjallarhorn to alert the Aesir, who prepared for battle. Using his magic Odin brought Mimir's head to life and sought counsel from it. Mimir advised the gods to fight on the Plain of Vigrid, a hundred leagues long and a hundred leagues wide, and to give their own lives if necessary to ensure that their enemies met utter destruction.

Surtur led his forces up Bifrost, intending to set Asgard itself afire, but the Rainbow Bridge broke beneath their weight, so they joined the giants and other monsters on Vigrid. The gods and einherjar came forth to meet them, and the clash of the two armies shook the Nine Worlds.

Wolves Pursuing Sol ("Sun") and Mani ("Moon") by J.C. Dollman. (Ivy Close Images / Alamy)

Odin made straight for Fenris. But prophecy held true, and before he could hurl Gungnir the monstrous wolf lunged forward and swallowed him whole. Thus the All-Father, wisest of gods, perished. But his son Vidar immediately avenged him. With his enormous boot he pinned the wolf's lower jaw to the ground, then used his great strength to take hold of Fenris's upper jaw and tore his gullet in two.

The other gods fared little better. Thor slew Jormungandr, but the Midgard Serpent's last venomous breath caught him in the face; he staggered back nine steps and died. Loki and Heimdall, bitter enemies for years untold, killed one another; Garm and Tyr likewise took one another's lives. Surtur killed Frey, who had only a weapon made of a stag's antler to fight with since he gave away his magic sword to win Gerd as his bride.

Soon the battle was all but over. Surtur, joyous in victory, cast his fire over all the world, and soon the conflagration burned so fiercely it slaughtered him, the jotuns, and everyone left alive on Midgard. Skoll and Hati caught up to the Sun and Moon and swallowed them, plunging the world into darkness just as the floodwaters closed over it for good.

But at the last moment, both the Sun and the Moon gave birth to daughters who could take their place in the sky. And a green, beautiful new world rose from the waves. Deep in Hoddmimir's Wood, two people, the woman Lif and man Lifthrasir, had survived by hiding under the bark of trees. From them descended all the people who soon inhabited the new world.

The only gods to survive Ragnarok were Odin's sons Vidar and Vali, Thor's sons Modi and Magni, Hoenir (who returned from Vanaheim to join his kin), Njord, and Baldur and Hodur (who returned from Hel). But nothing was left for them to do, and in time they, too, passed away, becoming nothing but the stuff of myth and legend.

Odin: Beyond The Eddas

While Odin is best known to us through the mythological and cosmological tales of the eddas, he also appears in many Norse sagas and legends. Most of his appearances occur in *konungasogur* (kings' sagas) and *fornaldarsogur* (tales of pre-Christian Iceland often featuring the supernatural). He is less likely to appear in *riddarsogur* (Norse romances that often take place in southern Europe) or *Islendingasogur* (Icelandic family sagas), except in brief references or mentions in verse.

Brynhildr pleads with Odin. (Mary Evans Picture Library / Alamy)

The Volsungasaga

One of the most popular Norse sagas is the *Volsungasaga*, the tragic tale of the hero Sigmund and his son Sigurd. Found in sections in many places (including the *Poetic Edda*), it forms the basis for the medieval German poem *The Nibelunglied*, which in turn inspired Richard Wagner's "Ring Cycle" operas. A full recounting of this enthralling epic is beyond the scope of this book, but several episodes within the greater story feature Odin.

Odin and Brynhildr

Brynhildr, daughter of King Budli, became a valkyrie and grew high in Odin's favor. He taught her more of the runes of power than the other valkyries, and gave her a cloak of swan's feathers so she could transform herself into a swan and fly down to Midgard. But despite this she defied him. Old King Helmgunnar went to war against King Agnar, whom Brynhildr loved. Odin told her to give the victory to Helmgunnar, but she instead helped Agnar triumph.

Odin kisses Brynhildr, his favourite Valkyrie, before imprisoning her on earth. (PD)

Odin's wrath when he learned of this was great, but Brynhildr came before him with unflinching courage to receive her punishment.

"You have gone against the Aesir, and so you may no longer live among us," the All-Father said. "I banish you to Midgard, where you shall sleep until one comes to claim you for his own."

"I ask only this, Ruler of the Gods," Brynhildr said. "Let it be that none save the most courageous of men, the greatest hero in all the world, shall win me for his wife." And out of his love for her, Odin granted her wish.

Odin placed in Brynhildr's flesh a thorn from the Tree of Sleep. He carried her sleeping form to Hindarfjall, a castle built of black stone by ten dwarves, and laid her on a couch. Then he caused a wall of flame to burn eternally around the castle, so that only the bravest of the brave would dare to approach the place. And so Brynhildr slept, awaiting her rescuer.

Odin and Hreidmar

One day, Odin, Loki, and Hoenir decided to take the form of men and walk among the mortals of Midgard. As they rested beside a river Loki saw an otter and maliciously killed it with a thrown stone. He made a bag of the beast's skin.

Soon the gods came to a house with two smithies and obtained hospitality there. When Loki boasted of slaying an otter, the head of the house, Hreidmar, snatched the bag from Loki's belt and examined it carefully. Then he told his sons, Regin and Fafnir, to seize the strangers, for Loki had slain Otr, their brother, whom Hreidmar had enchanted into animal form to provide food for the family.

"Hold, Hreidmar," Odin said. "It's true we killed your son, but we did so unwittingly, without knowing he was a man. Let us recompense you for his death."

"What recompense do you offer?" asked Hreidmar.

Now Odin's great wisdom failed him. He could have offered Hreidmar many things: a visit to Asgard, a drink of the magic mead, some wonder forged by the dwarves, a valkyrie wife. Instead he said, "Gold."

"If you bring me enough gold to fill this bag and to cover every single hair on the outside of it, I will accept it as ransom for your lives."

That worried Odin, for to meet Hreidmar's terms required a great amount of gold. Only one treasure in the Nine Worlds would suffice. He took Loki aside and whispered to him. "Know you of Andvari's hoard?"

Loki did. Andvari was a dwarf who had obtained a vast treasure from the river-maidens. He hid it in an underwater cave and protected it by taking the form of a pike. A shadow of grim evil seemed to lay upon the hoard, so no one had ever tried to steal it before, but Loki gladly did so. He caught Andvari and forced him to resume dwarven form.

"I will never give you my gold!" Andvari said. "I will go before Odin and demand justice!"

"Ah, but Odin sent me here to take it from you," Loki said.

Andvari, recognizing the truth of Loki's words, despaired, and gave in. Andvari tried through guile to keep back one item, a magic ring that had the power to create more gold. When Loki took it from him and put it on his own finger, Andvari cursed the ring, saying that evil would come to Loki and anyone else who possessed it.

Loki took the gold back to Hreidmar's house. After filling the bag he heaped gold over the skin. At last he used up all of Andvari's hoard, but still one hair remained uncovered.

"The ring on your finger, Loki, put that on the hair," Odin said. With ill grace Loki did so, and thus the gods ransomed themselves for Loki's wicked deed. But Andvari's curse held true. Soon Fafnir murdered his father for the hoard and transformed himself into a great dragon to protect it. Regin began dreaming and scheming about how to kill Fafnir and claim the treasure for himself.

The Volsungs

Odin had a mortal son, Sigi. Although he was a hero, Sigi committed an evil deed; he killed his thrall Bredi, who had done better than him while hunting. Branded an outlaw, Sigi fled south with Odin's help, and, in time, he became the king of Hunaland. When he grew old and weak his wife's brother murdered him and seized his throne, but his son Rerir avenged him and took the throne back.

Rerir and his wife had no sons, so they prayed to Odin and Freya for offspring. The gods sent Hljod, daughter of the giant Hrimnir, to bring a magic apple to the queen. After eating it, she became pregnant. During her term Rerir, while away at war, took ill and died. The queen remained pregnant for six years, at last giving birth to Volsung. He became king of Hunaland, despite his youthfulness, and in time a great warrior and hero.

In the north Volsung had a hall, the Branstock, built around an enormous oak tree of the same name. He married Hljod and had 11 sons, the eldest of whom was Sigmund, and one daughter named Signy.

Siggeir, king of the Gauts (Goths), sought Signy's hand in marriage. But when he visited, she thought him

Odin in disguise plunges a sword into a tree at the wedding of Siggeir and Signy. (Ivy Close Images / Alamy)

A 19th-century wood engraving by Karl Ehrenberg depicting the war between the Aesir and Vanir. (INTERFOTO / Alamy)

deceitful and evil, and did not wish to become his wife. Ten of Volsung's sons said she should marry him, but Sigmund agreed with her. Volsung decided that since they knew nothing evil of Siggeir, the marriage must take place.

During the wedding feast, a stranger entered the Hall of the Branstock, a man tall and broad-shouldered, barefoot, with but one eye. He wore a spotted cloak, tight-knit linen breeches, and a slouched hat. He had an air of age and wisdom, and no one dared approach him. From beneath his cloak he brought out a wondrous sword whose brightness lit the Hall. He thrust the blade into the Branstock up to the guard and said, "He who draws this sword from this tree shall have the blade from me as a gift, and he shall prove that he never carried a better sword in his hand than this." Then he left as mysteriously as he had come.

Volsung hospitably gave Siggeir the first chance to draw the sword, but the king of the Gauts failed. So in turn did Volsung and his ten youngest sons. But when Sigmund placed his hand upon the hilt, the sword, Gram, came forth almost effortlessly. Siggeir offered to buy it from him for three times its weight in gold, but Sigmund scornfully refused, earning himself even more of Siggeir's hatred.

Some time later, Siggeir lured the Volsungs to his land. He treacherously slew all of them save Sigmund, who escaped with the help of his sister Signy. Sigmund and Signy had a son, Sinfjotli, who helped his father kill Siggeir and avenge the Volsungs.

Sigmund encountered Odin twice more. The first was when Sinfjotli died. In the guise of a ferryman the All-Father met the grief-stricken Sigmund as he carried his son's body, took the corpse aboard his boat, and sailed away. The second encounter resulted in Sigmund's own death. Late in life Sigmund married Hjordis. Not long thereafter he went to war with King Lyngvi. The two sides seemed evenly matched, but then a stranger strode onto the battlefield, a tall and broad-shouldered man, wearing a blue cloak, the left side of his face obscured by his hat and hair. With his spear, he struck Gram, breaking the blade in two. Deprived of his wonder-weapon, Sigmund soon fell victim to King Lyngvi. But Hjordis, who was pregnant, saved the pieces of the sword.

Years later Sigmund's son Sigurd reforged Gram and used it to slay the dragon Fafnir and claim his hoard, thus bringing upon himself Andvari's curse. After that he found and rescued Brynhildr, setting in motion a further chain of events that would result in his death and many others, but Odin played only a slight part in those events. First, he appeared to Sigurd as "an old man with a long beard" to help him choose his horse Grani, of the blood of Sleipnir. Secondly, in the guise of an old man named Hnikar he joined Sigurd's expedition against King Lyngvi and offered Sigurd good counsel. Third, as Sigurd prepared to slay Fafnir, "an old man with a long beard" appeared and advised him to dig several pits to hide in so that Fafnir's blood would not scorch or drown him.

The Ynglinga Saga

In addition to writing the *Prose Edda*, Snorri Sturluson also wrote a much longer book called the *Heimskringla*. Dating to approximately AD 1230, it chronicles the history of the kings of Norway. Its first section, known as the *Ynglinga Saga*, describes the legendary Ynglings, whom Snorri believed later generations euhemerized into the Norse gods.

According to this account, many peoples lived in the cold lands of the north, and giants and dwarves as well. Flowing out of the mountains to the far north was the River Tanais (the Don River), once known as Vana Fork, which divided Asia from Europe. The land west of Vana Fork became known as Vanaheim, or Vana Home, because a people called the Vanir lived there.

The land east of Vana Fork was the home of a people who called themselves the Aesir. From their great city, Asgard, ruled a mighty chieftain named Odin. Handsome, strong, and eloquent, he taught his people many skills and ruled them well. Powerful in magic, prophecy, and shapechanging, he possessed many of the abilities and objects attributed to him in the eddas, such as two intelligent ravens who flew around the world gathering information for him.

King Odin was as mighty a warrior as he was a magician; he emerged victorious from every battle he fought. He laid hands on the heads of his men (many of whom were berserkers) and blessed them before each battle so that they had full faith they would win. If they ever found themselves in great difficulties they called on him by name.

Odin traveled extensively and owned vast lands in the south. Whenever he was gone his brothers, Vili and Ve, ruled in his stead, and his wife Frigg patiently awaited his return.

Odin attacked the Vanir, but for once could not claim victory. The tide of war shifted again and again, with no clear winner, and the battles devastated the land. At last the two sides chose to make peace and exchanged hostages. The Vanir sent Njord the Wealthy, his son Frey, and his daughter Freya (a priestess who first taught the Aesir the magic of the Vanir), and clever Kvasir to Asgard. The Aesir sent Hoenir, with wise Mimir to help him. The Vanir made Hoenir a chieftain, but when they discovered he wasn't very smart, they felt cheated in the exchange. So they cut off Mimir's head and sent it back to Odin. He preserved it with magic so he could bring it back to life and seek Mimir's counsel when necessary.

Knowing from his prophetic powers that his descendants would live in the northern lands, Odin left Vili and Ve in charge of Asgard and led the Aesir to Saxland (northwest Germany). There he took over much land, built a large temple, and gifted great estates to his sons and chief lords. These included Thor, Heimdall, Njord, Frey, and Baldur; the names of their estates correspond to the names of their respective halls in the standard Norse cosmology. He sired many other sons, and from them descend all the great kings and heroes who came after him.

For all his powers, Odin was still a mortal man, and at long last he felt death approaching. So he had his warriors stab him with a spear, saying he would go to join the gods and ever after all who died in battle would come to him. They burned his body on a great pyre, in accordance with the funeral rites he himself had established.

Odin and King Aun

Chapter 25 of the *Ynglinga Saga* describes a dark relationship between Aun, a wise and peaceful king of Sweden who is "a great believer in sacrifices," and Odin. At age 60 Aun sacrificed one of his sons to Odin, asking to have a long life. Odin told him that he would live another 60 years. When that period ended, Aun sacrificed another of his sons, and Odin said Aun's life would continue as long as Aun sacrificed another son to him every ten years. By the time he'd sacrificed his ninth son, Aun couldn't leave his bed and could only drink from a horn as if he were a baby. He wanted to sacrifice his tenth and last son, but the Swedes forbade it and so King Aun at long last died.

ODIN OF TROY

The *Ynglinga Saga* isn't the only manuscript where Snorri Sturluson describes Odin as a man who came from the south. In the *Prose Edda*, Snorri writes that Thor was a son of Priam of Troy, and that one of Thor and Sif's descendants was Voden or Odin, "an excellent man because of his wisdom and because he had every kind of accomplishment." Through his gift of prophecy Odin knew he would become famous in the northern lands, so he led his people north from Turkey and they settled in Saxland. In time Odin continued northward, leaving his three sons – Veggdegg, Beldegg (Baldur), and Sigi (ancestor of the Volsungs) – to rule over different parts of Saxland.

Odin settled in Denmark, of which he made his son Skjold the king. From him the Skjoldungs, the royal family of Denmark, takes its name. Odin continued northward to Sweden, where King Gylfi heard about "these Asians, who were called the Aesir." Because peace and prosperity followed the Aesir wherever they went due to their intelligence and beauty, Gylfi offered Odin power in his kingdom. Odin built the town Sigtun and, in the Trojan tradition, established a council of 12 men to "administer the law." Then he headed onward to Norway, where he made his son Saeming a king; he is the ancestor of all the Norwegian kings. Odin's son Yngvi became a king in Sweden; the Ynglings descend from him.

The Saga of King Hrolf Kraki

Hrolfs saga kraka, usually translated as *The Saga of King Hrolf Kraki*, chronicles the life and adventures of the eponymous warrior and his family, the Skjoldungs of Denmark. Composed sometime around AD 1400, it relates events that occurred about a thousand years prior. Odin appears in the tale to test Hrolf and his men to determine whether they can overcome the challenges awaiting them at the court of King Adils of Sweden.

King Hrolf went on a journey with his 12 champions, 12 berserkers, and 100 warriors. They came to the farm of a one-eyed man named Hrani. He invited them to spend the night, promising plenty to eat and drink despite their numbers. When they awoke the next morning it was bitterly cold in Hrani's hall. All the men got dressed quickly except for the king's champions, who felt comfortable in what they already wore. Hrani said, "If you think this cold is difficult to bear, you won't survive the hardships King Adils will inflict upon you." He advised Hrolf that a large force wasn't what he needed to defeat Adils, so he should send home half his men. Hrolf did so.

Hrolf and the remaining men rode on, and soon came to another farm where Hrani greeted them and offered hospitality. When they woke up the next morning an intense thirst afflicted them. Most of them rushed to the wine-vat and drank their fill. Again Hrani told King Hrolf that this was a sign of weakness, and that Adils would confront them with far greater challenges.

A storm sprang up, so Hrolf and his men stayed with Hrani another night. The farmer built a fire so intense that everyone but the king and his 12 champions backed away from its heat. Hrani advised Hrolf to send home all his men except the champions, or else he'd never defeat Adils. Hrolf, impressed with Hrani's wisdom, did so.

Hrolf and his 12 champions went on to avoid the traps King Adils set for them and defeat him. As they returned home they again came to a farm where Hrani greeted them. He offered Hrolf war-gear – a sword, shield, and mail – but Hrolf refused them due to their ugliness. Angered by this dishonor, Hrani told Hrolf he wasn't as wise as he thought. Hrolf and his men continued traveling without staying the night. They soon realized that one-eyed Hrani must be Odin and rode back, but the farm had vanished. They continued on to Denmark, not wanting to go to war again for fear that, by offending Odin, they had ruined their chance to ever win another battle.

The Saga of Olaf Tryggvason

Olafs saga Tryggvasonar, a part of the *Heimskringla* that Snorri derived from some earlier sagas of the same name, tells the story of King Olaf of Norway (ruled 995–1000), who helped to convert the Norwegians to Christianity. Part of the saga describes how Odin came to visit Olaf one night. He appeared as a wise, knowledgeable old man with one eye and a deep hood pulled low over his face. King Olaf "found much pleasure in the guest's speech" and stayed up late conversing with him. Every time the guest finished one tale, Olaf wanted to hear another. A bishop had to point out how late it was twice before Olaf went to sleep.

The king awakened in the middle of the night and told his servants to bring the guest to him, but they couldn't find him anywhere. In the morning, Olaf called his cook and cellar-master before him and asked if they'd seen the guest. The cook replied that when he began to prepare that day's meal a man he didn't know came to him, insulted the food, and offered two thick sides of beef, which the cook had prepared with the rest of the meat. King Olaf instructed him to destroy all that food, for clearly the guest was the heathen god Odin, "but Odin shall not deceive us."

In another version of the story, *The Separate Saga of St. Olaf*, Odin appears to King Olaf and gives the name Gestr ("Guest"). They speak of earlier kings, and Gestr pressures Olaf to say which of them he'd like to be, if he could. Olaf insists he'd never want to be any heathen man, but eventually names Hrolf Kraki. Gestr asks why Olaf wouldn't prefer to be other kings of great power, the implication being that Gestr could make him just such a king. Olaf, realizing that Gestr is "the evil Odin," thinks about hitting him in the head with his book of hours.

Sorla Thattr, from an expanded version of *Olafs saga Tryggvasonar*, also features Olaf and Odin. It describes Odin as the king of the Aesir and ruler of the land of Asiaheim. Odin curses two heroes, Hogni and Hedinn, to fight

A fanciful depiction of Olaf Tryggvason raiding along the coast of the English Channel. (North Wind Picture Archive / Alamy)

eternally, even returning from death to continue fighting, until a Christian man enters the battle and kills them. King Olaf accomplishes this in the first year of his reign.

The Gesta Danorum

Odin also appears in euhemerized form in the *Gesta Danorum* ("Deeds of the Danes" or "The Danish History"), a 12th-century chronicle written by Saxo Grammaticus. The first nine of the Gesta's 16 books cover the earliest "history" of Denmark, and thus sometimes touch on fantastic or legendary subjects related to Norse mythology.

In Book Six Saxo states his argument that the Norse "gods" were simply men in even starker terms than Snorri does:

At one time certain individuals, initiated into the magic arts, namely Thor, Odin and a number of others who were skilled at conjuring up marvellous illusions, clouded the minds of simple men and began to appropriate the exalted rank of godhood. Norway, Sweden and Denmark were ensnared in a groundless conviction, urged to a devoted worship of these frauds and infected by their gross imposture. The results of their deception spread, so that all other realms came to revere some kind of divine power in them, believing they were gods or the confederates of gods. They rendered solemn prayers to these wizards and paid the respect to an impious heresy which should have gone to true religion.

Hading's Adventures

In Book One of the *Gesta*, Hading (Hadding, Hadingus), son of King Gram, found himself alone in the wilderness after a monstrous giant killed his lover Harthgrepa. Odin appeared to Hading as an old, one-eyed man. He sponsored a friendship between the Danish prince and the pirate Liser (or Lysir). The two made war against Loker, king of Kurland, but he defeated them. Odin rescued Hading, took him to his home, "refreshed him with the aid of a soothing potion", and offered prophetic advice about how he could escape from Loker. Odin then returned Hading to where he found him. As they rode back, Hading peeked out from beneath Odin's cloak and was amazed to see

BELOW / OPPOSITE
Hading spies Odin on the shore. (Ivy Close Images / Alamy)

that the horse (Sleipnir) was running over the sea. Later, Hading slew King Svipdag of Sweden and became king of that country.

The warlord Uffi, eager for vengeance on the man who'd slain his grandfather Svipdag, proclaimed that he would give his famously beautiful daughter as wife to whoever killed Hading. A warrior named Thuning decided to try for the prize. As Thuning's fleet headed toward him, Hading noticed an old man on the shore – obviously Odin, even though Saxo doesn't mention the usual distinguishing features – signaling that he wished to come aboard. Against the advice of his crew Hading landed and let the old man board. Not only did the old man teach him a superior way to form his troops for battle, he used magic to counter Thuning's own attempt to gain an advantage through sorcery. After giving Hading some sound advice, the old man departed as mysteriously as he'd appeared.

Odin of Byzantium

Saxo then relates that there lived at that time a man named Odin, widely believed throughout Europe to be a god, who often dwelt at Uppsala. To honor him and show their piety the "kings of the north" made a statue of him out of gold and sent it to Odin's chief city, Byzantium. Odin was delighted, but his wife Frigg wanted to take the gold from the statue to make jewelry for herself. Odin prevented this by hanging the smiths who worked for her, and then "by a marvelous feat of workmanship" made the statue able to speak when touched.

Frigg began an affair with one of her servants, who cunningly arranged for the destruction of the statue so she could get the gold. Humiliated by both his wife's conduct and the ruin of his idol, Odin went into exile. In time, when he felt he had regained his fame and divine reputation, he returned to Byzantium. He discovered that Frigg had died and an evil magician, Mithothyn (possibly "False Odin"), had deceived the people with false gods and cults. Mithothyn fled before Odin, who dispersed the cults and re-established his own rule/divinity.

OVERLEAF
Odin rides with the Valkyries.

Other Mentions Of Odin

The text of the *Gesta Danorum* mentions Odin in several other places.

Book Three names Odin as the father of Balder, a "demi-god" said to suffer no harm from weapons, who lusted for a beautiful woman named Nanna. His enemy Hother, who wanted to marry Nanna, went on a quest to obtain a magic sword that could wound Balder. The two rivals met in battle, with "Odin, Thor, and battalions of deities" fighting alongside Balder. When Hother cut the handle of Thor's club in two, the gods lost the battle and fled. Hother married Nanna, but the conflict between him and Balder continued, eventually encompassing a struggle for the kingdom of Denmark. After two defeats Hother escaped into the wilderness, where a group of mysterious maidens told him how to defeat Balder. Following their advice, Hother snuck into Balder's camp and inflicted a lethal wound on him.

Odin learned of a prophecy that Rind (or Rinda) would bear him a son to avenge Balder. Using his *seidr* magic and trickery, Odin raped her. The other gods, perceiving that Odin's conduct had brought dishonor upon them, exiled him for ten years and made Oller (Ullr) their leader. Upon his return Odin became more powerful and glorious than ever. His son by Rind, Bo or Bous, killed Hother in battle but died of his own wounds.

In Book Seven, Odin favors a warrior named Harald Wartooth because of his height, strength, and handsomeness, so he granted him the power "that no sword could impair his safety[.]" In return Harald promised Odin the soul of everyone he killed in battle. After Harald became king of Denmark, the Swedes declared war against him, and he sought to learn more from the oracles. He met a tall, one-eyed, old man dressed in a shaggy grey cloak. Identifying himself as Odin, the old man taught Harald a special wedge formation that allowed him to defeat the Swedes.

Later Harald's trusted messenger Bruni drowned while on a journey. Odin took Bruni's form and "carried out a deceitful embassy" so that war resulted. Still disguised as Bruni, Odin served the aged, blind Harald as his charioteer. When the king realized who Bruni was, he begged Odin to grant victory to the Danes. Unmoved by this plea Odin threw Harald out of the chariot and then killed him with his own sword.

Some time thereafter the Hellespontines attempted to take a castle of the Danes. The witch Gudrun helped them by blinding the Danes, thus making it a simple matter for the enemy to get inside their castle and begin hacking them down. But Odin, who favored the Danes this time, appeared and lifted the spell so they could fight back. When the Hellespontines used magic to protect their bodies from weapons, Odin taught the Danes how to crush them with stones. In the end the two armies destroyed one another.

Starkad

Odin also interacts with the (in)famous hero Starkad. *Gautrek's Saga*, the

Hervarar Saga, and Book Six of the *Gesta Danorum* chronicle Starkad's life. Odin's involvement is best described in *Gautrek's Saga*, from which the story told here is primarily derived.

Starkad, who was unusually tall and strong because he had giants as his ancestors, was raised by Harald the Agder-King as his foster son alongside his own son Vikar. When King Herthjof of Hordaland killed Harald and took Vikar hostage, one of Harald's men, Grani Horse-hair, took Starkad in as his foster son. Starkad stayed with Grani until he was 12 years old, at which point he was as large as an adult and already growing a beard.

Vikar recruited Starkad and several other skilled warriors to avenge Harald's death. Thanks to their might and skill they soon did so, and after Herthjof's death Vikar became ruler of Agder and Jaederen. Vikar and Starkad went on to conquer many lands until Vikar was a rich, powerful king.

One day Vikar sailed north from Hordaland with a large army, but the fleet soon found itself trapped by storms in a small archipelago. Divination told the fleet's leaders that the storms would persist until they honored Odin with a human sacrifice chosen by lot. They cast lots several times, and Vikar's name always came up. The leaders of the army chose to sleep on the matter and make a final decision the next day.

That night Grani Horse-hair woke Starkad up and took him to another island where 11 men seated on thrones awaited them. There Grani revealed himself to be Odin, and the other men the Aesir. They declared that they would determine Starkad's fate.

Thor, who disliked Starkad because of his giantish blood, spoke first. "Starkad shall have no children, no line of descendants to follow him."

Odin, who favored Starkad, began granting him gifts. "Starkad shall live three times as long as a normal man."

Thor responded, "But he shall commit an evil deed in each of his three lifetimes."

Thor, son of Odin and god of thunder and storms, by ªRU-MOR.

"Starkad shall possess great wealth, and the best of weapons and clothing," Odin said.

"But never shall he own land, or receive any satisfaction from his possessions," countered Thor.

"Starkad shall have victory in every battle he fights, and great renown shall be his," said Odin.

"But his opponents will grievously wound him in each battle," Thor said.

"Great eloquence I confer on Starkad, and the ability to compose fine verse as fast as he can speak," Odin said.

"He shall never remember any of the poetry he creates," said Thor.

For Starkad's last gift, Odin said, "All the highest and most noble men of the land shall hold a fine opinion of Starkad."

"But all the common people will despise him," said Thor.

The famous illustrator Arthur Rackham depicts Odin in his traditional wandering garb. (PD)

With that the meeting ended and Odin took Starkad back to Vikar's camp. He said that Starkad should repay him (Odin) for the lavish gifts he had received, and Starkad promised to do so. Odin told Starkad to find a way to send King Vikar to him. He gave Starkad a spear that would appear to other men to be nothing but a reed.

When morning arrived, the leaders of the army decided to hold a mock sacrifice of King Vikar, hoping that would satisfy the demands of prophecy but spare Vikar's life. While Vikar stood on an old stump, Starkad placed a noose made of a calf's entrails around his neck and attached it to a branch he had bent down. When Starkad released the branch it sprang up swiftly, the noose became strong and tight around Vikar's neck, and the old stump fell away from his feet. Starkad stabbed Vikar with the "reed," saying, "Now I give you to Odin." Thus Vikar died, and forever after the common people hated Starkad for murdering their king.

Half's Saga

Halfs saga ok Halfsrekka ("The Saga of Half and His Heroes") provides a different account of Odin's interest in Vikar. King Alrek had two wives who didn't get along, so he decided to keep the one who brewed the best ale. Odin, disguised as "Hood," helped Geirhild win the contest. He spat on her yeast, saying he would take as payment what was between her and the ale-cauldron. Since she was pregnant, that meant her son, Vikar. Alrek chose Geirhild, but drinking the Odin-enhanced ale gave him a prophetic vision that Vikar would be sacrificed to Odin.

Hervarar Saga: Odin's Riddle-Game with King Heidrik

Hervarar Saga tells the story of the magic sword Tyrfing and how it affects the lives of many heroes, particularly the shieldmaiden Hervor and her son Heidrik. It includes an appearance by Odin.

After Heidrik became king, he sent word to one of his chief enemies, Gestumblindi, to appear before him and be reconciled, or lose his life. Gestumblindi knew this meant either submitting to the judgment of Heidrik's wise men, or defeating Heidrik in a riddle contest. He didn't like his chances, for he'd committed many crimes and knew he wasn't as wise as the king. He sought Odin's help. Odin told him to conceal himself, took Gestumblindi's form, and went to King Heidrik.

A depiction of the three gods Loki, Odin and Hoenir, from an 18th-century Icelandic manuscript. (PD)

When Heidrik offered him the choice of judgment or riddles, "Gestumblindi" opted for riddles. He then asked the king 29 riddles, each of which Heidrik answered without hesitation. For the 30th riddle Odin asked the same one that foiled Vafthrudnir, "What said Odin in the ear of Baldur before he was borne to the fire?"

This confirmed Heidrik's suspicions about "Gestumblindi's" true identity. Enraged, he drew Tyrfing and attacked Odin. The All-Father changed shape into a hawk and flew away. But before he left, Odin made a dire pronouncement. "Because you have attacked me, Heidrik, you shall die at the hands of the lowest of thralls." And so it soon came to pass when nine slaves murdered Heidrik in his sleep and stole Tyrfing.

Odin as Raudgrani

Orvar-Odds Saga ("The Saga of Arrow-Odd"), written in Iceland in the 13th century, tells the story of Oddr, a hero who's the subject of a dire prophecy. During his adventures he has an unusual encounter with Odin despite his persistent refusal to offer sacrifices to the gods or even believe in them. (At one point in the saga, Oddr says of himself and his men, "we believe in our own power and strength, and we don't believe in Odin.")

During his adventures Oddr met an unusual man who called himself Raudgrani ("Red-Beard"). They swore blood brothership, and Oddr did likewise with Raudgrani's foster brothers Gardar and Sirnir. Oddr desired revenge against Ogmund for slaying his blood-brother Thord. Raudgrani repeatedly tried to dissuade him by describing Ogmund's monstrous heritage and magical powers, but Oddr remained determined to avenge Thord.

After an inconclusive encounter with Ogmund, Oddr learned from Raudgrani that Ogmund had married Geirrid daughter of Geirrod. Oddr sailed to Geirrod's stronghold and attacked. Gardar died in the fierce battle, but Ogmund escaped by plunging into the earth after Sirnir and Oddr badly wounded him. When they returned to their ship they discovered that Raudgrani had vanished for good, and Oddr concluded he was none other than Odin.

Odin made another appearance as Raudgrani in *Bardar saga Snæfellsass* ("The Saga of Bard the Snow-God"), written in the 1300s. Specifically described in this story as one-eyed, he joined several other characters aboard a ship, where he expounded upon pagan worship and sacrifice at great length. This so angered a Christian priest that he hit Raudgrani in the head with a crucifix. Raudgrani fell overboard and was never seen again, and the men on the ship realized their companion must have been Odin.

ODIN THE GOD

To the Norsemen Odin wasn't a figure of myth and legend, he was their god, with the power to reward or punish as he saw fit. Capable of bestowing great favor on his worshippers, he could also capriciously withdraw his protection from someone if it suited his purposes, regardless of that follower's piety or the richness of his sacrifices.

Unfortunately information about the actual worship of Odin is relatively slim. Furthermore, it's difficult to say how and to what extent Norse religious practices differed from region to region, and over the centuries. The worship of Odin (and other Norse deities) seems to have been far less uniform than the term "religion" tends to imply to the modern mind.

Roman commentators, such as Tacitus in his *Germania*, typically equate Odin (or Woden) with Mercury, and increasingly with Mars as time passes (which may imply that Tyr/Tiwaz once enjoyed greater prominence, but Odin gradually supplanted him as a battle god). The identification with Mercury seems to derive from Odin's role as a wandering god, a god of magic/learning, and a god of the dead/psychopomp – all attributes associated with Mercury. Other sources, including AEthelwerd's *Chronicle*, refer to men in continental Germany or England offering sacrifices to Woden in the hope of achieving victory in battle.

While the worship of Thor or Tyr may have a lengthier pedigree, the worship of Odin seems to have achieved a certain prominence over time, perhaps in part because it appealed to the ruling/warrior classes. Based on place names and other evidence, some scholars believe Odin worship was prevalent in most of Scandinavia (particularly in Denmark and eastern Sweden) and the continent. The Icelanders favored Thor, but worship of Odin wasn't entirely unknown there. In fact, according to some sources Odin is mentioned more in early Icelandic literature than any other god.

Temples to Odin

Tacitus writes that the Germans of his time had no temples or idols; they worshipped their gods in sacred groves. Many other sources also refer to the use of sacred groves by the men of the North. However, Tacitus does mention an actual temple for the fertility goddess Nerthus and another famous temple the Romans destroyed.

As building skills improved, the number of actual temples in Germanic lands increased. For example, Bede describes the destruction of heathen temples in England, and mentions others that Christians converted into churches. Early Norwegian laws and some literary passages refer to complete, roofed buildings. Based on place names, some of these may have been dedicated to Odin or other specific gods, while some served more general purposes of worship.

According to Adam of Bremen's *Gesta Hammaburgensis Ecclesiae Pontificum* (*Deeds of the Bishops of Hamburg*), written in the 11th century, Uppsala in Sweden was the site of one of the grandest and most important Norse temples. "[E]ntirely decked out in gold" and encircled by a "golden chain," the temple contained wooden statues of three gods seated on a triple throne: Thor ("the mightiest") in the center; an armed and armor-wearing Odin (Woden) to one side; and Frey (Fricco) to the other. Here priests appointed to each god made sacrifices to them. Next to the temple was a sacred grove that featured a well and one particularly large evergreen tree of unknown species. But while Uppsala was undoubtedly of great importance as a sacred site, modern scholars do not take Adam's information entirely at face value. They think his report has at least some factual basis, but are uncertain to what extent it's based on unreliable sources or outright fabrication.

Other famous temples mentioned by Snorri Sturluson or in other sources include ones at Hladir and Maerin in Thrandheim, and one at Gudbrandsdal in central Norway. But the Uppsala temple was "the most glorious" and "the last bastion of northern heathendom," in the words of E.O.G. Turville-Petrie.

The *Landnamabok* describes temples in Iceland. The law specified a certain number of public temples per quarter, each supported with dues paid by local landowners. (Private temples also existed.) Every temple had an altar, on which it was required to keep an arm-ring weighing no less than two ounces. Legal and business oaths were sworn on the arm-ring, and the *godi* (a priest who was also a local secular lord) wore it on his arm at local assemblies.

A stone from Sweden depicting Odin on Sleipnir. (Photograph by Berig)

Sacrifices to Odin

Mortals often sacrificed to Odin to seek his favor. While animals (particularly horses, bulls, and boars) were the most common sacrifices, in the sagas the sacrifice was often a man. The most valuable human sacrifice was a fighter captured in war (particularly, according to the sixth century chronicler Procopius, the very first captive from a battle).

The primary methods of sacrifice to Odin described in Norse literature are hanging, burning, and piercing or marking the body with a spear at the time of death.

A mid-19th-century depiction of Odin enthroned with his ravens and his wolves. (PD)

Sometimes a rite included two or more of these methods. Adam of Bremen describes both men and animals hanging from the trees in the sacred grove at Uppsala. The custom of hurling a spear over an enemy army and dedicating their deaths to Odin, or even just slaying a specific enemy in battle – "giving him" or "sending him" to Odin – may also have constituted a form of "human sacrifice." Men slain in battle were sometimes said to "become Odin's guests" or "enjoy Odin's hospitality."

The Norse offered sacrifices at specific times or places according to tradition. The most important of these were at the start of winter (for plenty), at mid-winter (to increase the crops), and at the start of summer (for victory in war). The summer victory sacrifice was probably the one most directly connected with Odin (the other two were more associated with Frey and Thor, respectively).

According to Adam of Bremen, the priests at Uppsala sacrificed to Thor to stop plague or famine, to Odin in the event of war, and to Frey when a marriage took place. Furthermore, great sacrifices took place there every nine years at around the time of the vernal equinox. For nine days the priests sacrificed one man and two animals (such as dogs, horses, hawks, or roosters) each day, then hung their bodies in the nearby sacred grove. Other chronicles describe similar every-nine-years sacrifices at Leire in January.

But not all sacrifices were necessarily planned or scheduled. Some of the ones portrayed in Norse literature were more spontaneous. For example, the *Ynglinga Saga* describes how the inhabitants of Vermaland blamed a famine on their king, Olaf, because he rarely sacrificed to Odin. So they surrounded his house and set it afire with him in it, declaring the king a sacrifice to the All-Father for a good harvest.

Archeological discoveries have revealed another form of sacrifice. The ancient Scandinavians would cast valuable objects into bogs, which at least in some instances they seem to have done to honor Odin (and possibly other deities) as the god of battle. They carefully placed weapons, armor, shields, and other goods in bogs, typically after breaking them or otherwise rendering them useless.

Drinking to Odin

Many sources refer to the tradition of dedicating a cup of the best drink to Odin at feasts, festivals, and rites. If this were not done, bad luck would result and crops might fail. For example, in *Hakonar saga Goda* ("The Saga of Hakon the Good") in the *Heimskringla*, the "ardent heathen worshipper" Earl Sigurd held a great sacrifice of animals followed by a feast. At the feast men carried a "sacrificial beaker" (or goblet) around the fire. After that, "Odin's toast was to be drunk first – that was for victory and power to the king – then Njord's and Frey's, for good harvests and for peace."

Later, when King Hakon tried to convert the people to Christianity the farmers became upset. Earl Sigurd negotiated an agreement between king and people, and invited Hakon to his beginning of winter sacrificial feast. At the feast Sigurd toasted to Odin, but Hakon made the sign of the cross over the horn before drinking from it himself. To keep the peace Sigurd told the farmers this was the "sign of the hammer" and that Hakon had dedicated the drink to Thor.

Modern Worship of Odin

While the worship of Odin and other Norse gods is thought to have faded away in the centuries following the introduction of Christianity into northern Europe, some efforts have been made since the early 1800s to revive his faith. Known in general terms as Germanic Neopaganism or Asatru, and when more specifically directed at Odin as Odinism, this religion enjoys official recognition in several European nations. It has taken various forms in different times and places, including the Odinic Rite, the Odinist Fellowship, the Odin Brotherhood, and others. These organizations sometimes work more or less together, but at other times argue over terminology, practice, and authenticity.

ODIN IN MODERN CULTURE

Although not as popular or well-known in the modern day as his hammer-wielding son Thor, Odin nevertheless has survived into present times in various aspects of popular culture.

The Marvel Comics Odin

When Stan Lee and Jack Kirby transformed the god Thor into a comic book superhero in *Journey Into Mystery* #83 (August, 1962), it was inevitable that other elements of Norse mythology would also make their way into what would eventually be known as the Marvel Universe. One of the earliest was Odin. Some aspects of his personality and background track eddic myth closely; comic book writers remove or change others, and add many new ones, to suit the demands of the Thor storyline. For example, in the comics Odin stops Ragnarok from occurring.

Sir Anthony Hopkins as Odin from the 2011 Marvel film *Thor*. (AF Archive / Alamy)

As portrayed in the comics, Odin is one of the most powerful entities in the Marvel Universe. In various stories he stops time, transports all of humanity to another plane of existence, battles cosmically powerful beings such as the planet-eating entity Galactus, and blasts enemies on Earth with lightning while in Asgard. His power derives from the *Odin Force*, which has sometimes been taken from him by his enemies, or has passed into other beings, including Thor. He must periodically recharge it by entering the *Odinsleep*, a state in which he's as vulnerable as a mortal. In some eras of the Thor storyline Odin possesses the *Odinsword*, a gargantuan blade. Drawing the Odinsword from its scabbard signifies that the end of the universe approaches.

Disturbed by Thor's fascination with Midgard and her people, Odin has on several occasions stripped Thor of some or all of his powers (and sometimes full knowledge of his identity) and exiled him to Earth to learn humility. Fortunately Thor's heroism, honor, and nobility always help him win his way back into Odin's good graces. Odin frequently mediates disputes between his true son, Thor, and his foster son, Loki, who is Thor's greatest nemesis.

In the 2011 film *Thor* and its 2013 sequel *Thor: The Dark World*, Sir Anthony Hopkins plays the part of Odin. Much as in the comics he's a secondary character compared to his thunder god son, but his banishment of Thor to Earth is crucial to the development of Thor's character.

J.R.R. Tolkien based much of the look of his famous wizard Gandalf on the old stories of Odin when he travelled on earth. (Photos 12 / Alamy)

Odin in Fantasy Literature

Unsurprisingly, Norse mythology in general, and Odin in particular, have inspired many modern fantasy authors. For example, Jim Butcher's long-running *Dresden Files* series of novels features Odin as the one-eyed Donar Vadderung, a business executive who's powerful enough to easily defeat the protagonist, wizard Harry Dresden. He has assistants named Hugin and Munin. *The Long Dark Tea-Time of the Soul*, the second of the "Dirk Gently" novels by Douglas Adams, posits that gods no longer worshipped by humans become impoverished, possibly even insane. Odin is a man living in an asylum who trades away his divine power for clean bed linens.

The Works of J.R.R. Tolkien

Scholars have known for years that J.R.R. Tolkien drew on various northern European mythologies and tales as inspiration for his fantasy epics. For example, the One Ring that Bilbo finds in *The Hobbit* and whose destruction motivates the characters in *The Lord of the Rings* was inspired in part by the story of Andvari's magic ring in the *Volsungasaga*.

The image of Odin influenced Tolkien when he created Gandalf the Grey, the wizard who leads the characters in both the books mentioned above. In a letter dated December 7, 1946 (nine years after publication of *The Hobbit* but eight years before publication of *The Lord of the Rings*) he mentions having received some character illustrations that he didn't care for. Specifically he says, "Gandalf [is shown as] a figure of vulgar fun rather than the *Odinic wanderer* that I think of..." (emphasis added). In the grey-garbed, bearded, hat-wearing, staff-carrying Gandalf it's not hard to see Vegtam the Wanderer come to life once more.

Neil Gaiman's American Gods

Neil Gaiman's award-winning novel *American Gods* features several ancient deities in the modern world. The most prominent of these is Odin, referred to as "Mr. Wednesday." His powers (and those of other gods, spirits, and legendary beings) have diminished as worship of them faded. New gods inspired by American obsession with mass media, movie stars, high technology, and the like have arisen. Mister Wednesday urges the other Old Gods to join him and fight the New Gods, but has little success at first. Only after the New Gods murder Mr. Wednesday do the other Old Gods realize the true extent of the threat and unite to battle their enemies. Unfortunately it turns out that Loki is manipulating events behind the scenes so he can gain power from the chaos of the conflict, while the battle will serve as a sacrifice to restore Odin's power. It's up to Odin's son, Shadow, to defuse the situation and save the world.

Wagner's "Ring Cycle" Operas

Generations of opera lovers have gotten to know Odin as Wotan, one of the main characters in *Der Ring des Nibelungen* ("The Ring of the Nibelungs"), a cycle of four operas composed by Richard Wagner in the mid-19th century. Wagner derived the elements of his story from various Norse sagas, particularly the *Volsungasaga* and its Germanic parallel, the *Nibelunglied*.

Taking place over the course of approximately 15 hours, the Ring Cycle operas tell the story of a magic ring forged by the dwarf Alberich with gold he stole from the Rhine Maidens. Wotan, with the help of Loge (Loki), steals the ring, but Alberich places a death-curse on it. Wotan has to give the ring to the giants Fafnir and Fasolt to pay them for building Valhalla, but then desperately tries to regain the ring in various ways. His grandson Siegfried eventually obtains it by slaying Fafnir (who himself killed Fasolt to have sole possession of it), but dies as a result of the schemes of Alberich's son Hagen. His lover, the fallen valkyrie Brunnhilde (Wotan's daughter, whom he stripped of her immortality for trying to save Siegfried's father Sigmund) returns it to the Rhine Maidens and then rides into Siegfried's fire. Hagen tries to get the ring but the Rhine Maidens drown him. The epic concludes with fire consuming Valhalla and the gods.

Odin in Games

Given the popularity of Norse mythology in general, it's not surprising that it – and Odin – are featured in many modern games.

Odin appears in several tabletop roleplaying games ("RPGs"). Many RPG supplements, such as *GURPS Vikings* (Graeme Davis; Steve Jackson Games, 2002), look at Norse culture in general for gaming purposes. As part of that they describe Odin and the rest of the Aesir in sufficient detail for gamers to represent

Singer Wilhelm Rode as Wotan in *Die Walkure*, the second part of Wagner's famous opera. (INTERFOTO / Alamy)

them accurately in game sessions. The role of Odin becomes even more important in RPGs specifically focused on playing in the style and setting of Norse mythology, such as *Fate of the Norns: Ragnarok* (Andrew Valkauskas; Pendelhaven, Inc., 2013).

The most detailed treatment of Odin in RPGs to date is for *Dungeons & Dragons*. It includes in its library of game materials the book *Deities & Demigods*, which describes numerous gods and heroes from world mythology for use in D&D. The 1st Edition rules' version of the "DDG" (1980) ranks Odin as a 30th level cleric, 14th level druid, 18th level ranger, 30th level magic-user (wizard), and 15th level bard with 400 hit points; Gungnir is a +5 spear that inspires fear in all nearby enemies. By the time of the 3rd Edition of the game and its more detailed rules for divine figures (2002), the rules describe Odin as a divine rank 19 (out of 20) god with 980 hit points who qualifies as a 20th level fighter and 20th level wizard with numerous special powers, abilities, and immunities. In either case he's not someone to be trifled with.

Appearances by Odin in board and card games are less common, but not unknown. For example, in the cooperative board game *Yggdrasil* (Ludonaute, 2011), the players take on the roles of Odin, Thor, Freya, and other Norse gods as they work together to stop the encroachment of Loki, Fenris, and other monsters. Odin's insight and wisdom grant him the power to draw two Enemy cards instead of one, choose one of them, and put the one he likes less on the bottom of the deck. Similarly, the collectible card game *Yu-Gi-Oh!* features a "Storm of Ragnarok" expansion set with an "Odin, Father of the Aesir" card that has significant powers.

Numerous video and computer games incorporate elements of Norse culture. For example, a game might feature settings that visually draw on the Vikings for inspiration, or allow players to play character archetypes such as a Berserker, Valkyrie, or Skald. But only a few games feature Odin or other gods in any meaningful way. In the real time strategy game *Age Of Mythology*, Odin is one of the "major gods" who can grant a player special technologies, units, and powers. In the action roleplaying game *Too Human*, the gods are actually a technologically advanced society of cybernetically enhanced beings. ODIN (Organically Distributed Intelligence Network) is the artificial intelligence who created them and infused them with runic power; Hugin and Munin use their bionic eyes to observe things for it.

BIBLIOGRAPHY

Primary Sources

Many of these tales and sagas are available online in various editions and formats from websites such as the Icelandic Saga Database or Project Gutenberg. You may find it helpful to add "English" to the search term, since editions in the original Old Norse, or in modern Scandinavian languages or German, are common. Quotes in this book from the *Poetic Edda* are from the translation of Henry Adams Bellows, which is available online.

Bellows, Henry Adams. *The Poetic Edda* (The American-Scandinavian Foundation, 1923)

Byock, Jesse, trans. *The Saga Of King Hrolf Kraki* (Penguin Books, 1998)
    —*The Saga Of The Volsungs* (Penguin Books, 1990)

Evans, David, ed. *Havamal* (Viking Society for Northern Research, 1986)

Hollander, Lee, trans. *Old Norse Poems* (Columbia University Press, 1936)
    —*The Poetic Edda* (University of Texas Press, 1962)
    —*The Skalds* (University of Michigan Press, 1968)

Larrington, Carolyne, trans. *The Poetic Edda* (Oxford University Press, 1996)

Lassen, Annette. *Hrafnagaldur Odins* (Viking Society for Northern Research, 2011)

O'Connor, Ralph, trans. *Icelandic Histories and Romances* (Tempus Publishing Ltd., 2006)

Orchard, Andy, trans. *The Elder Edda: A Book Of Viking Lore* (Penguin Books, 2011)

Palsson, Hermann and Paul Edwards, trans. *Gautrek's Saga And Other Medieval Tales* (New York University Press, 1970)
    —*Seven Viking Romances* (Penguin Books, 1985)

Penguin Group. *The Sagas Of The Icelanders: A Selection* (Penguin Books, 1997)

Ryder, G. Frank, trans. *The Song Of The Nibelungs* (Wayne State University Press, 1962)

Saxo Grammaticus. *The Gesta Danorum* (also titled *The Danish History*) (various editions available)

Sturluson, Snorri (Arthur Brodeur, trans.). *The Prose Edda* (Pacific Publishing Studio, 2011)
    —Byock, Jesse, trans. *The Prose Edda* (Penguin Books, 2005)
    —Faulkes, Anthony, trans. *Edda* (Everyman, 1987)

–Hollander, Lee, trans. *Heimskringla: History Of The Kings Of Norway* (University of Texas Press, 1964)

–Young, Jean, trans. *The Prose Edda: Tales From Norse Mythology* (University of California Press, 1954)

Tolkien, Christopher. *The Saga Of King Heidrik The Wise* (also known as the *Hervarar Saga*) (Thomas Nelson and Sons, 1960)

Secondary Sources

Abram, Christopher. *Myths of the Pagan North: The Gods of the Norsemen* (Continuum International Publishing Group, 2011)

Acker, Paul and Carolyne Larrington, eds. *The Poetic Edda: Essays On Old Norse Mythology* (Routledge, 2002)

Adam of Bremen (Francis Tschan, trans.). *History of the Archbishops of Hamburg-Bremen* (Columbia University Press, 2002)

Andren, Anders, Kristina Jennbert, and Catharina Raudvere, eds. *Old Norse Religion In Long-Term Perspectives* (Nordic Academic Press, 2006)

Auld, R.L. "The Psychological and Mythic Unity of the God Óðinn." *Numen* 23 (1976), 145–60.

Bayerschmidt, Carl and Erik J. Friis, eds. *Scandinavian Studies: Essays Presented To Henry Goddard Leach* (University of Washington Press, 1965)

Carpenter, Humphrey. *The Letters Of J.R.R. Tolkien* (Houghton Mifflin Company, 1981)

Chadwick, H.M. *The Cult Of Othin* (Cambridge University Press, 1899)

Chadwick, Nora. *Anglo-Saxon And Norse Poems* (Cambridge University Press, 1922)

Clover, Carol and John Lindow, eds. *Old Norse-Icelandic Literature: A Critical Guide* (University of Toronto Press, 2005)

Clunies Ross, Margaret. *Prolonged Echoes, Vol. 1: The Myths* (Odense University Press, 1994)

Davidson, H.R. Ellis. *Gods And Myths Of Northern Europe* (Penguin Books, 1964)

–*The Lost Beliefs Of Northern Europe* (Routledge, 1993)

–*Myths And Symbols In Pagan Europe: Early Scandinavian And Celtic Religions* (Syracuse University Press, 1988)

–*The Road To Hel* (Cambridge University Press, 1943)

DuBois, Thomas. *Nordic Religions In The Viking Age* (University of Pennsylvania Press, 1999)

Dumezil, Georges. *Gods Of The Ancient Northmen* (University of California Press, 1973)

Fleck, Jere. "Odinn's Self-Sacrifice – A New Interpretation: I. The Ritual Inversion." *Scandinavian Studies* 43 (1971), 119-42; "II. The Ritual Landscape," 385-413.

Glendenning, R.J. and Haraldur Bessason, eds. *Edda: A Collection Of Essays* (University of Manitoba Press, 1983)

Jakobsson, Armann. "A Contest of Cosmic Fathers: God and Giant in *Vafthrudnismal.*" *Neophilologus* 92 (2008), 236-277
  –"Odinn as Mother: The Old Norse Deviant Patriarch." *Arkiv för nordisk filologi* 126 (2011), 5-16

Kershaw, Kris. *The One-Eyed God: Odin And The (Indo-) Germanic Mannerbunde* (Journal of Indo-European Studies Monograph No. 36, 2000)

Lassen, Annette. "Odinn in Old Norse Texts Other Than *The Elder Edda, Snorra Edda,* and *Ynglinga Saga.*" *Viking and Medieval Scandinavia,* Vol. 1 (Brepols Publishers, 2005), 91-108

Liberman, Anatoly. "A Short History of the God Odinn." *Nowele* 62/63 (October 2011), 351-430

Machan, Tim, ed. *Vafthrudnismal,* 2nd edition (Pontifical Institute of Medieval Studies, 2008)

McKinnell, John. *Essays On Eddic Poetry* (University of Toronto Press, 2014)

McTurk, Rory, ed. *A Companion To Old Norse-Icelandic Literature And Culture* (Blackwell Publishing, 2007)

Owen, Gale. *Rites And Religions Of The Anglo-Saxons* (Dorset Press, 1985)

Polomé, Edgar, ed. *Old Norse Literature And Mythology* (University of Texas Press, 1969)

Rankine, David. *The Isles Of The Many Gods* (BM Avalonia, 2007)

Raudvere, Catharina and Jens Peter Schjodt, eds. *More Than Mythology: Narratives, Ritual Practices, And Regional Distribution In Pre-Christian Scandinavian Religions* (Nordic Academic Press, 2012)

Schorn, Brittany Erin. " 'How Can His Word Be Trusted?': Speaker and Authority in Old Norse Wisdom Poetry." Diss. Corpus Christi College, University of Cambridge, 2012.
  –"RE: Wisdom Poetry and Vafthrudnismal." Message to the author. May 29, 2014. E-mail.

Starkey, Kathryn. "Imagining an Early Odin." *Scandinavian Studies* 71 (1999), 373-392

Turville-Petrie, E.O.G. *Myth And Religion Of The North: The Religion Of Ancient Scandinavia* (Holt, Rhinehart, and Winston, 1964)
  –*Nine Norse Studies* (Viking Society for Northern Research, 1972)

Retellings of Norse Myths

Colum, Padraic. *The Children Of Odin* (Macmillan, 1920)

Crossley-Holland, Kevin. *The Norse Myths* (Pantheon Books, 1980)

Guerber, H.A. *Myths Of The Norsemen* (George G. Harrap & Co., 1909)

Reference Sources

Lindow, John. *Norse Mythology: A Guide To The Gods, Heroes, Rituals, And Beliefs* (Oxford University Press, 2001)

Orchard, Andy. *Dictionary Of Norse Myth And Legend* (Cassell, 1997)

Simek, Rudolf. *Dictionary Of Northern Mythology* (D. S. Brewer, 1993)

Online Resources

Germanic Mythology: http://www.germanicmythology.com/index.html

Icelandic Saga Database: http://sagadb.org/

Norse Mythology Online Library (part of the Norse Mythology Blog): http://www.norsemyth.org/p/books.html

Septentrionalia: http://www.septentrionalia.net/index.html

Viking Society Web Publications: http://vsnrweb-publications.org.uk/